BELLADONNA

BELLADONNA

Charlotte Grey

Chivers Press   •   G.K. Hall & Co.
Bath, England   Thorndike, Maine USA

_L-
F
GRE

This Large Print edition is published by Chivers Press, England, and by G.K. Hall & Co., USA.

Published in 2000 in the U.K. by arrangement with Robert Hale Limited.

Published in 2000 in the U.S. by arrangement with Robert Hale Limited.

U.K. Hardcover ISBN 0–7540–4008–9 (Chivers Large Print)
U.S. Softcover   ISBN 0–7838–8862–7 (Nightingale Series Edition)

The text of this Large Print edition is unabridged.
Other aspects of the book may vary from the original edition.

Set in 16 pt. New Times Roman.

Printed in Great Britain on acid-free paper.

British Library Cataloguing in Publication Data available

Library of Congress Cataloging-in-Publication Data

Grey, Charlotte.
     Belladonna / Charlotte Grey.
        p.   cm.
     ISBN 0–7838–8862–7 (lg. print : sc : alk. paper)
     1. Inheritance and succession—Fiction.   2. Large type books.
     I. Title.
     PR6057.R457 B45   2000
     823'.914—dc21   99–051868

CHAPTER ONE

It was nine months now since the old Earl of Barnstaple had died and been succeeded by his nephew, Richard Dunthrop. The new earl was just then in conference with his lawyer: an irritating situation, for there was nothing that Mr. Banstead of Banstead, Chipstead, Ashstead and Caterham had to say that the younger man could like to hear.

'I regret it, my lord, but, by the terms of the late earl's will, it is my duty to remind you that . . .'

'Yes, yes, yes!' Lord Barnstaple returned irritably; 'I know it well enough! And it does not seem any less monstrous to me now than it did when you first told me of it after my uncle's death.'

'The earl, your uncle, was anxious—most anxious—that the title should not die out.' Mr. Banstead's voice was placating.

'I am very well aware of it. Ever since the late war he tried by every means in his power to get me leg-shackled. Cajolery, flattery, anger, blandishments, disappointment, commands, pitiful pleading—there was nothing he did not use in an attempt to get me to the altar. The only thing he did not do was to cut me off with a shilling. He left that till after his death.' The earl ended on a bitter

1

note.

'It need not come to that, my lord. There are still three months left till the end of the year succeeding your uncle's death. You have plenty of time to find a pleasant, suitable female and marry her before the time is up.'

'But, dammit it, Banstead, I have no wish to marry!' Lord Barnstaple returned with a ferocious glare. 'And I hold you very much to blame!' he went on. 'You should never have agreed to draw up such a will.'

The lawyer spread his hands. 'I regret it, my lord. I tried to dissuade his late lordship, but, I assure you, he was adamant. If I had not agreed to do the work, his lordship would have gone elsewhere.' Mr. Banstead smiled in a fatherly fashion. 'I can understand very well how you feel, my lord, but, I can see his late lordship's point of view also.'

'I am perfectly well as I am! I have no wish to have a female interfering in my life!'

Ever since he had returned from the continent after the wars ended in '15, the earl, as Richard Dunthrop, had enjoyed a carefree bachelor life in London. True, his uncle had nagged him to marry in order to ensure the continuance of the title, but Richard had avoided every lure thrown at him, and had gone on his pleasant way, one of the most elegant, sought-after men in society. Now, by the terms of his uncle's will, he must give up his freedom and marry if he was to inherit the

2

monies and the estates that went with the title, but which had been entirely at the late earl's disposition.

'The season is but just starting, my lord!' the lawyer said now cajolingly. 'I have heard that there are some very agreeable fillies coming out this year.'

'I can see exactly how it will be!' the earl retorted testily. 'I shall be chased by every female with a yen to see her daughter a countess, and no doubt the chits themselves will be just as forward!'

'You have till the end of July, my lord,' Mr. Banstead said soothingly. 'There is no need for undue haste. Three months, after all, will enable you to look about comfortably.'

A sour glance was all the lawyer's reply.

*   *   *

'My dear, positively, he *has to* marry!' Lady Parton gazed at her crony, Mrs. Arbuthnot, with gleaming eyes and the air of one who has imparted a piece of intelligence of the highest significance.

Mrs. Arbuthnot's already rather protruding china-blue eyes looked as if they would pop entirely out of her doll-like head. 'Do you mean . . . ?' she breathed in awe.

'No, no, no! Of course not!' Lady Parton returned impatiently. 'There is nothing of that in the case.' She stopped and looked at her

3

friend suspiciously. 'Unless you have heard—?'

'*I* have heard nothing! I am quite dependent upon *you* for my information, dearest Letitia. Pray continue.' And Mrs. Arbuthnot leaned forward with a most gratifying display of eagerness.

'Well,' Lady Parton continued, mollified that she was to be the one to impart the news, 'it appears that the on-dit about Barnstaple is quite true. I have it on the best authority that he must marry before the season is over.'

Mrs. Arbuthnot sat back and smiled complacently. 'Well, if that is not good news— especially for you, dearest Letitia.'

Lady Parton's only child Marjory was still on the marriage market at twenty-three, and so far had had not the slightest success in attaching the interest of any parti, suitable or otherwise, as Mrs. Arbuthnot well knew. The news that such a died-in-the-wool bachelor as the earl of Barnstaple needed a wife was, therefore, bound to be of particular interest to her friend.

Lady Parton smiled graciously. Mrs. Arbuthnot was childless, and so no rival in this instance. She merely enjoyed the thrills of the season vicariously, through the successes or failures of her friends.

'Of course, you do mean to, I collect . . . that is . . . ? Mrs. Arbuthnot hinted delicately.

'Barnstaple would be very suitable,' Lady Parton acknowledged. 'His title is impeccable, and as soon as he inherits properly his late uncle's property, he will be one of the richest men in the country. Oh, yes; I do not think I should quibble over his lordship.'

Mrs. Arbuthnot gave an understanding smile. 'And how have you heard of this, Letitia, my dear? Oh, I know the on-dit has been circulating ever since the earl died, but Barnstaple was not in London for the little season, and no-one seemed to know *for certain* . . .'

Lady Parton hesitated a moment, then leant forward to whisper, 'My dear, it appears that it is the talk of Parton's club, and Frobisher, my own maid, you know, heard something from one of Barnstaple's footmen . . .'

Mrs. Arbuthnot nodded wisely. None knew better than she the value of a pretty lady's maid.

They continued to discuss the matter for some little time longer, then Lady Parton took her leave to plan her assault upon Lord Barnstaple, and Mrs. Arbuthnot departed to her own apartment to don her bonnet preparatory to calling upon some other of her friends to spread the good news and to listen to their designs.

*　　　*　　　*

The ball given by the Marchioness of Harn was attended by everyone who was anyone in

5

society. Of course Lord Barnstaple was amongst those who had received a card, but as he settled his waistcoat and selected a seal for his fob, he did not view the prospect before him with any enthusiasm. It was the first ball of the season, and he knew that already he was the talk of drawing-rooms and clubs, and that assaults would be made on him from every side. He knew that he would not be able to stand up with anyone without there being a deal of speculation that she was to be the new countess, and he would certainly be pressed to take notice of a great many young females in whom he had not the least interest.

The earl straightened his shoulders and took a deep breath before he entered the ballroom. He felt once again all the injustice of his late uncle's will, and thought sourly that so far he had never met a woman whom he could endure at his breakfast table for more than a few months.

Out of the corner of his eye he saw a formidable dowager bearing down upon him, and in her wake her rather plain daughter whose fashionable gown could do nothing to hide the pocked complexion and the indeterminate chin. Hastily the earl looked about him and spotted across the room an acquaintance to whom he made his way as fast as elegance and a fashionable, unhurried demeanour would allow.

As Katherine Netley watched her sister Susan being borne off by the Earl of Barnstaple, her heart jumped for joy. Now Sir James Brocket must ask her to stand up with him for the sets that were then forming, and she looked at him expectantly.

Sir James was speaking in a low voice to her father, Viscount Netley.

' . . . once or twice, I believe,' his lordship was saying.

Sir James frowned, and stared after Susan and the earl.

His look cut Kate to the quick, and she took a step forward so that she herself was in Sir James's line of vision. She smiled at him eagerly.

'Oh, Miss Kate, dare I hope that you will honour me with your hand for this dance?' Sir James said obligingly, with the smile that always turned her knees to jelly.

There was no happier girl in Lady Harn's ballroom than Kate Netley as she rested her hand on Sir James's arm and walked with him to the set. After all, she had been in love with Sir James for at least a year now, and still she hoped against hope that her feelings were returned. She could not hide from herself that there was something special in Sir James's look when he gazed at her sister Susan, but she refused to give up hope, and now, having

Sir James to herself, she smiled at him as charmingly as she knew how, and talked cheerfully, determined to make Sir James concentrate upon herself, and to stop his eyes wandering off to where Susan was standing opposite Lord Barnstaple.

But provokingly, Sir James would still talk about Susan. 'I collect that your sister has met Barnstaple before?'

'I believe that she danced with him occasionally last season.

Sir James paused and looked down the set. Then, with a visible effort, he said confidentially, his eyes amused, 'Just see how everyone is looking at them. I vow there is not a young lady here who would not change places with your sister.'

'I assure you, Sir James, there is *one!*' And Kate smiled meltingly.

'You are a kind creature, Miss Kate!' Sir James said, suddenly serious. 'But I daresay your sister is happy!'

'I—I do not know, sir!' Kate stammered, blushing, her heart abruptly in her slippers, stricken by the expression on Sir James's face, which left no doubt as to his true feelings.

'After all,' the baronet went on wistfully, 'Miss Susan is standing up with the most eligible gentleman in the room.'

But Kate was too stricken to contradict him. 'I do not know what Susan thinks of Lord Barnstaple, sir; we have never spoken of him.'

Now Sir James seemed to shake himself, and his usual lively smile returned to his face. 'What is this you tell me Miss Kate? That you two have never exchanged confidences about the earl! Come now; I can hardly believe that! When it is upon everyone's lips that he must marry at last: Richard Dunthrop who has escaped the net so far! Surely every female in London must hope to attach him now!'

Kate blinked back the tears pricking her eyelids. 'Not every female, sir!' she whispered.

Luckily it was their turn to dance down the set then, and Kate was spared the pain of having to listen to Sir James further. She could no longer close her eyes to the fact that it was her sister Susan who was Sir James's object, and for the moment, even dancing with Sir James himself was unable to lift her out of the dismals.

*　　*　　*

The Earl of Barnstaple's manservant tut-tutted sympathetically, and silently handed his master a fresh linen neck-cloth as yet another discarded effort fell crumpled to the floor. He watched anxiously as the first folds of the Trone d'Amour took shape under the earl's normally deft fingers.

The earl paused before making the all-important second tuck. With the utmost care he took the cloth between his fingers again, folded it gently and began to pass the other end through. The manservant watched the manoeuvre anxiously, willing success. But the fine adjustment necessary for perfection was lacking, and another failure hit the floor.

'Damnation!' his lordship exclaimed.

'Exactly sir—er—my lord,' the man amended quickly, having forgotten in his perturbation, his master's elevated status.

'I can not think what is the matter!' the earl declared irritably, knowing full well exactly what was the matter. Today was the day upon which he had decided to get leg-shackled at last, and the idea appealed no more now than it had ever done. He thought grimly of all the many attempts his late uncle had made to get him to marry. Now, with only two months and a few days to go before the year after his uncle's death was up, he was about to take the plunge and ask for the hand of the Honourable Susan Netley. He had danced with her several times since Lady Harn's ball; he had found her an amiable creature, and one who would not disgrace a countess's coronet. Moreover, she had not cast out lures.

The earl sighed as he thought of the gossip there had been already this season. He had always had a horror of gossip and scandal, ingrained ever since an unfortunate event which had happened in the earl's green days. Then he had been rescued from a compromising situation only by the efforts of

10

his late uncle, who had bought back the young man's letters, and also bought off the lady's husband—both very expensively. Since then he had always behaved with the utmost circumspection, and had cut short any acquaintance the moment the lady in question had begun to treat him in any sort of prorietary manner. A number of very fetching little ladybirds as well as greater ladies had found that it did not pay to attempt to cross the invisible line Richard Dunthrop had drawn round himself.

It was doubly galling to him therefore, to have been made the subject of gossip by the terms of his uncle's will. But when he was bethrothed, doubtless the gossip would die away. And, little as he cared to acknowledge it, the earl had to admit that his late uncle had been right. The Barnstaple earldom, old and honourable, should not be allowed to die out. And Susan Netley came of fertile stock: one of six children herself, her three married sisters were already following in their mother's footsteps.

Besides, he could not like the idea that the Barnstaple millions should go to some charity for the indigent mistresses of royal princes, which was where it seemed it would go if he did not fulfil the conditions of his uncle's will.

It was to such worries as these that his lordship ascribed his current inability to tie his neckcloth with his usual perfection. He took a

11

fresh piece of linen and began again.

But hardly had he made the first fold when there was a discreet knock at the door. His man, Jameson, opened the door and spoke to the footman, then turned back to his master. 'Mr. Borrowdale is below, my lord.'

'Oh—have him sent up,' the earl grated, desperately trying to save his new creation. As the door closed, he knew he had failed again, and he flung the linen down in disgust.

'Most regrettable, my lord,' Jameson said sympathetically.

'I almost had it then!' the earl responded. 'What the devil can Mr. Borrowdale want at this hour?' It was nearly mid-day.

The Honourable Simon Borrowdale's yellow head appeared round the door, his face stretched in its usual good-natured beam. But as his eyes encountered the havoc before him, the smile faded and his eyes grew round with astonishment, and he looked at his friend, his mouth agape.

'Good Lord, Dick!' he ejaculated. 'What *are* you about?'

'You can see what I'm about well enough!' was the earl's irritable reply. 'And for heaven's sake come in instead of standing there like a gaby, and tell me what you want at this God-forsaken hour!'

Unused to any annoyance making the earl less than polite—for he was known for his invariable good manners as for the perfection

12

of his garb, which was totally without anything of the dandy, in spite of the importance he attached to his neck-cloths—Mr. Borrowdale realised that something must be much amiss, and he came in quietly and closed the door softly.

'We had arranged to view some items at Christie's, had you forgot, Dick?' he said equably, seating himself and regarding his friend with decidedly concerned eyes.

'Damn it, I had!' the earl returned in his former manner. Then becoming aware of his friend's expression, he smiled wryly. 'I'm sorry, Simon. I did not mean to paste you, but, to tell truth, I'm devilish put out this morning.'

'So I must imagine,' Mr. Borrowdale returned, viewing the piles of crumpled linen on the floor. 'What's amiss, Dick?'

'I'll tell you soon enough. But first, I must concentrate on this.'

'What had you in mind?'

'The Trone d'Amour.'

Mr. Borrowdale's eyebrows rose. 'But that is not normally any trial to you!'

'It is this morning!'

'So I see. Well,' he added quickly, seeing that the earl was going to break forth into indignant, irritable speech once more, 'why not the Mathematical—?'

The earl's face now looked like thunder. 'The Mathematical—!'

'Or the American?' Mr. Borrowdale added

13

with diplomatic speed.

'I wouldn't be seen dead in it! It's fit only for the Colonies—or persons from Cornwall. Jameson, pray let us continue.'

'Of course, my lord.' Jameson handed another fresh cloth to his master, and the earl began yet another attempt.

Mr. Borrowdale sat silent, his hands resting on his stick, watching his friend with perturbed concentration. He saw that another failure was imminent and quickly averted his eyes.

The earl let out another expletive, then viewed his friend sourly. 'Well, don't just sit there, Simon! *Do* something!'

'Anything, Dick! I'm always ready; you know that.'

'Then help me with this damned neck-cloth!'

'If I might make so bold, my lord,' Jameson said hesitantly. He really could not help feeling exceedingly sorry for the earl to whom the most intricate patterns of neck-wear were normally but child's play. But this morning it was plain that there was something on his lordship's mind, and Jameson, as a good servant, had a very shrewd idea what it was.

The earl turned to his elderly man with something like hope. 'Of course, Jameson! You always did it for his late lordship, did not you?'

'Yes, my lord.' Jameson had been the late earl's man, and consequently had known the

14

present earl all his life, and had been only too glad to continue in the new earl's service, the latter's man having decided to retire upon reaching the age of seventy and being provided with a good pension.

With practised fingers Jameson settled the folds of cloth, reaching over the earl's shoulders and watching his own actions in the glass. The snowy folds mounted high in the exact formation of the intricate Trone d'Amour, and under his arms he could feel his master relaxing.

'You are a marvel, Jameson!' the earl smiled approvingly when the man had finished. 'Simon?'

'Superb!' Mr. Borrowdale said reverently.

'Now my waistcoat, Jameson.'

The man brought forward a discreet silk garment with tiny crimson flowers embroidered all over it.

The earl saw it, made to put his arms through the armholes, then demurred. 'I think not, Jameson,' he said in gloomy tones.

'*Not*, my lord!' Jameson prided himself on knowing exactly what his gentlemen would wish to wear without being told. Anxiously he regarded his master. The waistcoat he was holding now seemed to him to suit his lordship's circumstances exactly.

'No. I think I'll wear the grey, Jameson.'

'The *grey*, my lord?' This was a decided setback.

'The grey, Jameson,' the earl confirmed gloomily.

More concerned than ever, Jameson made the exchange.

Mr. Borrowdale had listened to this passage with concern. 'Pon my soul, Dick, what has come over you? You were well enough when I saw you last week before I left Town to visit m'Mater! What has befallen you since then? I don't like to say it, but you look more as if you were dressing for another funeral.'

'And so I am, Simon. So I am.' Despondently the earl slipped on the grey waistcoat and ordered the dark charcoal tail-coat to follow.

'Someone I have not heard about—since I went away?' Mr. Borrowdale ventured.

The earl shook his head, a pained and suffering look upon his countenance.

Mr. Borrowdale said nothing further, but watched the conclusion of the toilet with foreboding. It was clear that something very serious was up with his old friend, Dick Dunthrop, and he could best help by sitting tight and waiting for enlightenment, ready to offer what succour he could when Dick was ready to confide in him.

At last the coat had been smoothed over the earl's broad shoulders to his own and Jameson's satisfaction, the earl was handed his hat and cane, and proceeded from the room with heavy tread. Mr. Borrowdale rose and followed him. In the same silence they descended to the street and began to pace along the pavement. Mr. Borrowdale shuffled his feet to get into step, anxious to add no further irritation to his plainly much-disturbed friend.

'I am afraid that I shall not be able to accompany you to Christie's, Simon,' the earl said at last, his voice lugubrious. 'I could not concentrate. I have another, too-weighty matter on my mind to which I must attend before anything else.'

'I'm sorry to hear that, Dick,' Mr. Borrowdale sounded very solicitous. 'There's the Oriental porcelain from Petersfield Castle on view, and I had thought you meant to bid for some of it.'

'And so I did. So I did.'

The earl's gloom was oppressive, and the two men strode on in silence for a while, Simon following Richard's lead, which was in the direction of St. James's Park.

When they were beside the lake, contemplating the pelicans, Richard spoke again. 'I owe you an apology, Simon—and an explanation. I am sorry to break our engagement—which would be a deal pleasanter, I assure you, than that on which I must embark—but I must admit, because of this—this other matter, I did not recollect it! Otherwise, I should have—' The earl paused, and heaved a sigh.

17

Mr. Borrowdale gazed at his friend, his face bearing a suitable expression of concern and forgiveness.

'—have arranged it for a different time,' the earl concluded heavily.

'There's not the least need for you to offer me any explanation, Dick!' Simon said hastily. 'If other business has come up since I went away, I'm hardly going to fly up into the boughs with you because you have to attend to another matter. After all, we had made but a loose arrangement. After all, what's a friend for?' he went on somewhat awkwardly.

The earl cast his friend a grateful look, then turned back to his contemplation of the water-birds. 'I can't come with you, Simon, because I have decided that I've got to get it over with. I'm going to see Netley.' The last words came out as though a visit to the prince of Hades was being contemplated.

'Oh?' Simon sounded puzzled. 'You're— you're not in hock to him, are you Dick?' he asked diffidently, when the earl had been silent for some moments. He knew Dick gambled a good deal, and though he could not think that the earl's pockets could be to let, he could think of no other reason for his friend to visit the viscount.

'I wish it were something as simple as that!' the earl returned, his voice as dejected as was his face. 'No; I'm going to ask him for his daughter Susan's hand.'

Simon's eyes grew round again as he stared at his friend, and his mouth dropped open even further than it had when he had viewed the chaos in his friend's room earlier. 'Good Lord!' he breathed. Then more loudly. 'Good Lord! I say, Dick, old man, you are—er—I mean—you are—all right?'

Gloomily the earl proceeded to explain his reasons for this procedure. 'You recall, Simon, the provisions of my uncle's will. Well, I have scarce two months left. If I ask for Susan Netley now, we can be married before the end of the season without indecent haste.'

'But—I had thought you might ignore your uncle's condition, and let the money go hang?'

The earl shook his head gloomily once more. 'My uncle was right. I can not let the earldom die out. Besides, I can hardly be the earl of Barnstaple on the money left me by my mother. You've no idea how expenses have mounted since I inherited.' And the earl looked at his friend with mournful eyes.

Simon Borrowdale clapped the earl's shoulder in silent sympathy.

CHAPTER TWO

In his study in his house in Wimpole Street, Augustus, Viscount Netley, sat in his comfortable chair, feeling very well satisfied

19

with the world. With six daughters to get married, and deprived of the help of a wife, for Lady Netley had died an exhausted and disappointed woman some years before, he could not but feel extremely pleased to have his fourth daughter spoken for. Three girls had already left their father's home, and the prospect of a fourth soon to quit the parental nest was enough to warrant the viscount giving himself an extra glass of best port.

Sir James Brocket was a thoroughly estimable young man and would provide very well for Susan. He had a house in the country and a good ten thousand a year, and seemed to be head over heels in love with the girl. True, the viscount had first thought that Brocket was interested in his fifth daughter Kate, but of late Susan's blonde prettiness clearly had attached him more. His lordship hoped that Kate was not badly disappointed. He had a specially soft spot for Kate, who was the only one of all his daughters to take after her mother in looks, being dark-haired and rather taller than the other Netley girls, who were all blonde and petite.

Still, it was an excellent thing that Susan was settled. He supposed that she and Brocket would now be arranging matters between them. He must have a little word with Kate later, but now the viscount settled down to enjoy the feeling of a morning well spent.

He was decidedly surprised when a footman

arrived to say that the Earl of Barnstaple was desirous of seeing him. He knew the earl, of course; Netley had been a good friend of the old earl, and so had known Richard Dunthrop since he had been a child. Of late years, they had met frequently at Watiers, and the viscount liked the younger man, but could positively think of no reason why Barnstaple should wish to see him now. Still, he was at leisure, and there was no reason why he should be denied. Accordingly, therefore, he gave orders for the earl to be shown in.

Lord Barnstaple himself was feeling more uncomfortable than ever as he crossed the hall to Lord Netley's study. He ran over in his head how the conversation would go: a few minutes to pass the time of day; a few more on any subject that offered itself; then—the fewest of seconds to ask for Miss Susan Netley's hand, and then he would find himself irrevocably leg-shackled.

The prospect was no more appealing than it had ever been, and the earl felt as though he were walking to his execution outside Newgate. He pulled himself together with an effort as they reached the study door. After all, he could hardly turn back now; he had better face up to things squarely.

His host had not the least idea of these feelings as Lord Barnstaple entered the room as the footman held the door open for him. He saw only a sober-suited, but most expensively-tailored figure coming towards him with all the assurance of a leading figure in London Society.

Lord Netley rose to greet his visitor. 'This is a great pleasure, my lord,' he said very affably. He was somewhat taken aback as he saw more clearly the earl's unsmiling manner. He thought the visitor's face a decidedly Friday one, and wondered what on earth could be amiss.

'My lord.' Richard bowed formally, and took the seat Lord Netley indicated, and stretched a languid hand on the arm of the chair.

'I had imagined you would be at Christie's this morning, my lord,' Lord Netley said politely when his guest failed to utter a syllable. 'I had thought of going, but I was—er—delayed.'

'I had indeed thought of it, my lord, but—' And Lord Barnstaple's voice faded away.

'Quite so,' his host responded. 'Some excellent Chinese porcelain, I collect. But perhaps there was nothing there that would have enhanced your own renowned collection.'

Lord Barnstaple bowed his acknowledgements, and murmured that his host was very kind.

Lord Netley waited a moment for something further. Lord Barnstaple, who seemed to have fallen into a brown study, now roused himself to enquire after the viscount's own renowned collection of prints.

'I missed some Durer woodcuts last week,' the viscount responded regretfully. 'The banker Isaacson beat me to them. That fellow seems to have unlimited resources.'

The two spoke for a moment or two about the depredations in the saleroom of certain nouveaux riches collectors, the conversation for the moment slightly less stilted. But then Lord Barnstaple fell silent once more, and Lord Netley wondered why on earth his guest, usually so suave and at ease, was so much in want of words now. Now he came to look at him, he looked positively blue-devilled.

As for the earl, he heard his own voice, languid as ever when he spoke, but somehow his brain would not send his tongue words as it usually did. He took a deep breath, and forced himself to get to the point. 'I—er—I have a particular reason for calling upon you this morning, my lord,' he began, wishing he had rehearsed the interview more thoroughly.

Lord Netley waited expectantly, wondering what on earth could be coming.

Lord Barnstaple took a deep, silent breath as he approached the nub of his call. 'I have—er—during the course of the season—er—had the pleasure of coming to know your daughter, Miss Susan. I have—er—always found her a most pleasant and agreeable female.'

Lord Netley smiled his thanks, and sat up a little straighter, every sense alert now that he had at last a suspicion of why Barnstaple had asked to see him. He must wait a moment or two for some further words from the earl, but he thought he comprehended the younger man's discomfiture perfectly now.

Lord Barnstaple paused to take breath, his collar feeling unusually tight, but thinking that at least he had made a start, albeit without the finesse he could have wished for. He took an even deeper breath, and plunged again. 'As you know, sir, last year I inherited from my uncle . . .' He looked expectantly at his host.

'Yes, indeed. A sad loss. A sad loss. We had been friends for over sixty years.'

'You doubtless know, my lord, of his anxiety that—that there should be an heir. While he was alive,' suddenly Richard rushed on, hardly pausing for breath, 'I always felt that there was no need for me to take any action, but now, of course, the situation is changed, and I feel that I should—er—look to the future.'

In the speaker's ears, the words did not sound in the least loverlike, and he made another attempt. 'It has—er—as I have said, been my pleasure to be with your daughter, Miss Susan, upon several occasions, and I—er—flatter myself that your daughter is—er—that we agree together very well—'

Lord Netley, who had been regarding the earl with total astonishment as well as interest since he had started to make his declaration—for all London knew that Barnstaple was a

24

dyed-in-the-wool bachelor, who would never lead any woman to the altar—now broke in for, stilted as it was, the drift of Lord Barnstaple's remarks could no longer be mistaken. Not, at least, by anyone who was accumulating experience at the rate being achieved by Lord Netley. 'Excuse me, my lord, but before you say anything further, I feel that I must tell you that my daughter Susan is already spoken for.'

'Spoken for!' Lord Barnstaple stared, stupefied for the moment, not for one second having considered this outcome. Quickly, he forced his face to resume its usual languid look. 'You mean—!'

'Exactly so, my lord,' Lord Netley confirmed, nodding. 'Scarcely an hour ago.'

'An hour!' Lord Barnstaple felt he was repeating everything like the veriest gaby, but for the moment his mind was quite adrift, having been completely thrown off his track.

'Yes, indeed, my lord.'

Richard sat up even straighter. 'May I ask, my lord, who it is who has been before me?' he asked, surprise and growing annoyance making him sound extraordinarily censorious.

'Certainly, my lord. It is Sir James Brocket who has asked for my daughter Susan's hand. An announcement will appear in the Morning Post very shortly. There is no secret.'

'Brocket!' Richard frowned. From what he had observed, which admittedly had not been a great deal, he had always assumed that it was another of Netley's daughters who had been Brocket's object: the tall, dark one whom he believed was called Kate. Had he known of Brocket's interest he would never have considered the girl. To be beaten to the post—and by a mere baronet! Richard stared at his host haughtily.

'I greatly regret, my lord, but—' Lord Netley was apologetic. '—I collect that there has been mutual attachment there for some time.'

Richard sat staring for some moments, his mind going over again the last few occasions when he had been in Miss Susan Netley's company. Certainly, now he came to think of it, Brocket seemed always to have been there as well, but he had always assumed that the baronet's interest was in the other sister. It only went to show how very deceitful women were, and how wise he had been to have nothing serious to do with them!

He remembered how Susan Netley had gazed at him with her limpid blue eyes, as if butter wouldn't melt in her mouth. He had never for a moment thought that—Well! He had had a lucky escape now, and the best thing he could do was to take his leave at once.

Accordingly, he rose. 'Pray say no more, my lord,' he said grandly, though Lord Netley had given no indication that he meant to speak. 'I am very sorry—' His feelings of mingled relief and outrage showed in his voice; 'I regret—that I have been too late.'

Lord Netley rose also, thinking now what a pity it was that Barnstaple should have hit upon Susan. He did not think for one moment that his lordship's affections were engaged: if only he had decided upon one of the other girls—well, Kate, for of his remaining daughters, Charlotte was still in the schoolroom, and the others were already married and with families.

Lord Netley sighed. A connection with Barnstaple would have been very gratifying. Perhaps if he laid the seed—put the idea into his lordship's head. 'My two other girls, my lord—' he murmured hopefully; 'they are both still quite unattached . . .'

But Richard did not take the bait. Indeed, Lord Netley wondered if he had even heard what he said. 'Just so, my lord,' he remarked distantly. 'I regret infinitely that I have wasted your time.'

The viscount felt the opportunity had slipped from him, and said nothing further on that head, but pulled the bell. The two men stood in silence till the footman reappeared, when Lord Barnstaple bowed himself out.

Still feeling a good deal of indignation, he made his way to his club at the end of Pall Mall, flung himself into a chair, and ordered a brandy. He drained it at a gulp, and indicated that he needed a replacement. The well-trained waiter obeyed the behest silently, and Richard took it with a grunt, and disposed of that also.

He felt somewhat restored afterwards, and managed to enquire, 'Have you seen Mr. Borrowdale yet, Jenkins?'

'No, my lord. I fancy he has not yet arrived.'

'Let me know when he does.'

'Certainly, my lord.'

Left alone, Lord Barnstaple considered the fiasco of the morning. He had made an utter fool of himself, asking for Netley's daughter when Brocket had got there before him; and he acknowledged to himself that it was this circumstance that rankled with him more than his failure to achieve Susan Netley's hand. After all, he had never thought that he was in love with the girl.

The earl frowned as he considered what had occurred. To be foiled before he had even reached first base was the outside of enough, and it meant that he would have to begin all over again looking for a wife, and with time getting shorter every day!

He wished Simon Borrowdale would arrive. He longed to be able to confide his grievances into a friendly ear. They had arranged to meet at the club, but as his interview with Netley had been a good deal shorter than he had bargained for, he could hardly expect Simon just yet.

Richard sank still farther down into his

chair, and ordered yet another restoring brandy.

* * *

Kate Netley thought that the day was the most horrid she had ever known. She had heard Sir James arrive to see her father, and tried to persuade herself that he was come to ask for her hand. She waited on tenterhooks, hanging over the banisters, for a summons to her father's study, but when the summons came it was for Susan and not for herself

The celebratory dinner that evening was almost more than Kate could bear, and for the greater part of it she sat miserably watching the faithless Sir James sitting beside Susan and gazing upon her in a most odiously loverlike way, while beside her prattled her dull cousin, Marjory Parton, mooning about how wonderful Lord Barnstaple was, and did not Kate think he was the finest Corinthian in London.

* * *

After a night in which Kate wept a good deal, and concluded that her heart was irrevocably broken, she awoke the next morning to find things quite as horrid as they had been the previous day.

Sir James came round to Wimpole Street at an abominably early hour as was allowed in a received betrothed, and Kate had to endure the sight of Sir James and her sister flirting over the boiled eggs and kedgeree and mutton chops at breakfast!

This proceeding gave her such a disgust of the pair that she left the table before she had eaten half enough, and shut herself in her room, her bosom heaving with indignation, and vowing to herself to be revenged upon them both.

The most satisfactory, answer, she felt, would be for her to go into an early decline. Upon her deathbed she would forgive Sir James his perfidy, and die with a blessing upon her lips. *That* should heap coals of fire upon his head!

The insuperable difficulty about that proceeding would be that she would not be about to enjoy the effects.

Besides, it was all so horridly final.

And Kate did not feel in the least like going into a fatal decline. She cast about in her mind for a different revenge.

The only one that came to her was that she should make—and at once—a much better match, which would enable her to patronise her sister to her own comfort. It was while she was cogitating along these lines that she thought of the current gossip about Lord Barnstaple: how he had to marry to inherit his uncle's money, and the thought of the earl came to her like an answer to her prayer.

And the earl was decidedly devastating. He must be about thirty-five, and was a leader of the Corinthian set, and was generally considered very handsome.

Kate rose and went to inspect herself in the glass. She saw an oval face and dark brown hair which curled naturally about her temples, violet eyes, which normally danced with fun, but were now shadowed by reason of her broken heart. Her complexion was a delicate pink and white, and not marked in the least. Indeed, the only criticism which might be made of her person was that she was a little over tall. But in the present case, that would not matter for Lord Barnstaple was well over six feet in height.

She came to the conclusion that a countess's coronet would suit her very well. And, had she not been irrevocably in love with Sir James Brocket, she might well have fallen in love with Lord Barnstaple herself.

Certainly, if Lord Barnstaple needed a wife, she was the very person to suit him. It would be a most satisfactory marriage of convenience, and Lord Barnstaple should know of it at once.

Having no mother to scheme for her in the marriage market, Kate was quite prepared to plan her own schemes. Indeed, her three married sisters had had to do it for themselves, for their father had not the least idea of how to go about such things, and her aunt Parton would certainly not help; indeed, she would be more likely to take over any parti who appeared, having Marjory still on her hands, and there being no sign of any happy developments in that quarter.

True, she had bungled the matter of Sir James Brocket; but then, she had been in love with him, and emotion had clouded her judgement. But now that her feelings were not involved, she was certain that she would be able to deal more judiciously.

Kate stared at herself a little gloomily now. Her sisters were all fair and delicate-looking; they had only to gaze up at a man tremulously for him to be overwhelmed with the desire to protect them. But men did not feel like that towards Kate. And in a great many cases they had to look up to her.

After a good deal of cogitating, Kate decided that the best thing would be for her to put her proposition to Lord Barnstaple herself—straightforwardly, exactly as one business man would approach another with some financial scheme.

CHAPTER THREE

Kate Netley was a young woman of resolution and action. And now, as soon as she had decided what she should do, she set about planning how it should be done; and as soon as that had been decided, she at once set out to do it.

Her first idea was to wait till she met Lord Barnstaple in the course of the social round. This would not be difficult, for they were always at the same balls and receptions; she could easily contrive to take him aside at some such event and put her proposition to him.

But a little reflection convinced her that that was not the best milieu for such a delicate conversation. They might be overheard, and in any case, in such a situation she would, no doubt, have to fight for his attention with a score or more of other young women and their mammas, all intent on securing the eligible earl for themselves.

No. She must have an appointment with him when they would remain undisturbed.

That decided, Kate accordingly looked through her wardrobe for a garment suitable for the undertaking, meaning to proceed to action without delay.

After a good deal of further cogitation, she chose a pelisse-robe of mauve challis, with neat bows of a deeper shade down the front. Instead of the bonnet she normally wore with the dress, which was decidedly frivolous, she put on a rather plain leghorn hat, trimmed only with a quantity of cream ribbon. She judged it to be decidedly more business-like than the bonnet, and it had the advantage of shading her face. Gloves and a small reticule and pearl grey slippers completed the ensemble.

It was but a short distance from Lord Netley's house in Wimpole Street to the Barnstaple mansion in Cavendish Square, and Kate managed to slip out of the house unseen, and tripped along the pavement, praying that she would meet no acquaintance.

In less than five minutes, she had reached the square, and had pulled at the bell of the earl's front door. It was only then that Kate began to wonder how she should broach the subject to Lord Barnstaple; after all, it was not exactly the sort of thing a young woman said to any man, and the idea of flight was just about to present itself to her mind, when the door opened.

'I wish to speak with Lord Barnstaple upon a most urgent matter,' she said quickly. 'Miss Katherine Netley.'

The footman bowed, showed her to a small sitting-room, and retired, murmuring that he would see if his lordship was at home.

Kate sat on the edge of a chair, bracing herself to go through with what she had begun, not sure whether she wished Lord Barnstaple to be at home or not.

*   *   *

His lordship had just repaired to his library to peruse the morning paper. He was expecting

Simon Borrowdale to arrive shortly, and when the footman entered, he looked up, expecting his friend's arrival to be announced.

He was more than taken aback when he learnt that it was instead one of the Netley females who wished to see him. Katherine . . . Miss Susan Netley's sister, whom he had met several times, and whom he had supposed was the object of that wretched Brocket. What on earth could she want, coming to see him in this—very improper manner? Had there been some mistake over Miss Susan? None of the ideas that flashed through his lordship's mind seemed in the least likely, and he asked the footman to show in the visitor, not at all sure that he should not have denied himself

He watched Miss Katherine Netley enter the room. It was obvious at once that she was not in good spirits, for her violet eyes looked tired as she regarded him, and her whole face was decidedly drawn.

'It is very kind of you, my lord, to receive me,' she murmured.

'I am happy to be of service to you, Miss Katherine,' Lord Barnstaple returned, and offered her a chair.

The young woman took it composedly enough, and watched as the servant withdrew and closed the door. Then she turned back to her host and regarded him gravely for a few moments.

'Lord Barnstaple,' she said at last, 'I realize

that this must seem an unusual proceeding, but I have come to you upon a business matter.'

'Indeed, ma'am?' Lord Barnstaple regarded his visitor feeling more puzzled than ever. He knew that this Miss Netley was but eighteen, and could not think what she meant.

She looked at him now pitifully, and Lord Barnstaple's naturally kind heart was moved in spite of the unusual circumstances. 'If I can help you in any way, ma'am . . . ?'

The girl now plainly took a deep breath and forced herself to her task. 'Yesterday, my lord, I received such a shock as I think I shall never recover from.' And the huge violet eyes welled with giant tears.

'I am indeed sorry to hear that, ma'am.' Lord Barnstaple viewed his visitor with concern. It was a long time since any female had managed to melt him with tears, but he felt that in the present case, the tears were genuine, and he felt sorry for the girl. Accordingly, he pulled out his kerchief and offered it to her.

She took it with a muffled 'Thank you', applied it to her eyes, blinked, and after a good blow, quickly regained control of herself, as his lordship saw approvingly.

'I must be plain with you, my lord,' Kate went on, her voice at first a little unsteady, but growing stronger as she proceeded. 'I would beg only, that you will hear me out, my lord.

Please.'

Her host bowed. 'Of course, ma'am. I will wait until you have finished your whole story.'

'Thank you.' Kate paused some moments, gathering her thoughts. Then she braced herself, and eyed the earl without flinching. 'My lord, the situation is this. I had thought, until yesterday, that is, that I was—er—that a certain gentleman would—er—offer for my hand. In that I have been proved sadly mistaken, and I feel that—that I shall never be truly happy again.'

Lord Barnstaple realized, of course, that his visitor was speaking of Brocket, and was puzzled as to why she should be favouring him with her confidence. The recollection of Brocket brought back all his own offended feelings, and he was somewhat slow to protest that his visitor would recover in time.

Evidently the girl thought he was about to speak, for she raised one hand slightly, and looked at the earl in such a way as to remind him of his promise. 'I realize, of course, that in time the hurt will be less, my lord, which is doubtless what you would say, but—I can not think that, whatever may happen to me in the future, I shall ever reach the heights of felicity, and to that I am resigned.'

His visitor looked so dolorous that Lord Barnstaple was about to remonstrate, but Kate only paused to draw a quick breath before hurrying on.

'However, my lord, I have no wish to remain an old maid all my life; I hope sometime in the future to be tolerably happy once more, and I must add that I have every intention of making my husband, when I have one, a good, faithful and cheerful wife. My family is—er—not undistinguished, and my portion, though not munificent, is not negligible. I am in hopes, therefore, that a suitable arrangement may be made soon. I say soon, my lord, because I am convinced that it would be more agreeable to me to have my own establishment as soon as possible.'

Lord Barnstaple heard these words with growing amazement, still not in the least being able to imagine why Miss Katherine Netley should be confiding in him. He recollected his promise to observe silence till his visitor had finished, however, and made no comment, but merely regarded Kate with a good deal of open astonishment.

The girl noted this, and said quickly, 'I can well understand that you feel puzzled, my lord, but, in a moment, all will be plain.' Here she took a deep breath, and looked at the earl it seemed to him appealingly, though what she was appealing for, he was at a loss to understand.

'I collect, my lord,' she went on slowly after a moment, 'from—er—what I have heard—that—that—er—you are seeking a wife with some speed. I have always understood—er—

I collect that your affections are not—er—
engaged, and I thought, my lord, that as you
need a wife, and I want to be married, that it
would be a very suitable match if we were—
to—er—'

Kate stopped, and looked at Lord
Barnstaple, this time with desperate appeal.
His lordship stared back at her, amazement
fighting with his growing anger. It seemed that
Netley must have told her of his asking for her
sister, and now this chit had come to him to
propose herself in her sister's place! It was
beyond all things! He had never heard
anything like it in all his life! Besides, he
preferred blonde, delicate women. This young
hussy needed a good set-down, and he
proposed to give it to her forthwith.

But before he had gathered his thoughts
sufficiently to begin, his visitor was launched
into speech once more. 'Oh, I know how it
must sound to you, my lord, and I must confess
that it seems very odd to my own ears, but only
think how practical it would be! You need a
wife! I want a husband! And as the affections
of neither of us are engaged, I do not see why
we should not rub along together very well!
And I would promise not to be the least
trouble to you. I would not hang about you
and ask you where you had been or whom you
had been with, as I know many wives do. I
promise I would not be like that at all! I would
do my best to make you comfortable, my lord,

39

in every way within my power. And—and I am perfectly healthy, my lord!'

The astonished earl had not been able to get a word in edgeways, even if he would. Now he noted somewhat grimly that his visitor had at least had the grace to blush at her last words, and had just opened his mouth to utter the opening words of a very decided reproof, when Kate burst into words yet again.

'And if you wonder why I have come to you now, my lord, it is because I knew I could never speak to you undisturbed at any ball or reception. Every marriageable female is out to trap you, my lord. I know for a fact that my own aunt, Lady Parton, hopes to fix you for my cousin Marjory. By the way, I do not think you would care for Marjory much, my lord, but there may well be others that you like better. And—I did not want my own case to go by default! I mean, you might be snaffled up at any moment—'

Here Kate had to pause for breath again, and she stared at her host panting, with fierce eyes and heightened colour.

Lord Barnstaple had listened to Kate's declamation with increasing stupefaction and irritation. But, as the chit had continued, his anger had diminished and his hilarity had grown. By the time she ended, he was listening to her with a broad smile upon his face.

'It is all very well for you to laugh, my lord—' Kate began indignantly.

'You—ridiculous child!' Lord Barnstaple burst out, unable to repress his laughter. 'What are you thinking of!'

'I am not a child, my lord! This is my second season, as you must know, and I can tell you that I have shown remarkable steadiness, for from my very first ball, I have been interested in only one person, and had he not yesterday asked for my—for someone else, I should not be here now! I am not one of your giggling neophytes, my lord!'

'I am sorry, Miss Katherine, but—you must admit that the situation is unusual' Still Lord Barnstaple could scarce restrain his laughter, though he made a valiant attempt out of respect for his guest's susceptibilities.

'But are not the circumstances unusual, my lord!' Kate now demanded with some asperity. 'It is not everyday that a man *needs* to find a wife . . .'

'And what makes you think that *I* am in that situation, ma'am?'

'It is well known in London that by the terms of your uncle's will, my lord—' Kate began, then stopped and regarded his lordship with something like horror. 'Oh, my lord!' she breathed. 'You mean I am too late?'

The words brought back all the earl's feeling of injustice and distaste, and for a moment he frowned. But then the absurdity of the present situation struck him again and he allowed himself a chuckle. 'No, Miss

41

Katherine, you are not too late, in that I do not yet have a wife,' he remarked good-naturedly.

'Well, then. . .' Kate said reasonably.

Lord Barnstaple regarded her in silence for some moments, sighing resignedly to himself. His uncle had put him in a damnable position, laid open, as he now was, to chits like this young Netley girl proposing themselves for his hand. But then he thought what a fool he had made of himself at this girl's age; when one was young, one was impatient—one did things without thinking. So, when he spoke again, Lord Barnstaple's voice and look were kind.

'Do not you think, ma'am, that it would be better for me to—to choose my own wife—in the usual way? Come, Miss Katherine, I see that you must agree—'

'I am aware, my lord, that I have not behaved in accord with convention, but, as I said before, I was anxious that my proposal should not go by default. Having no mother, my lord, I have to make shift for myself in many ways. And, you must agree, it would be a most suitable arrangement . . . and Kate regarded his lordship hopefully.

The earl regarded the flushed face in front of him, thinking that he had never seen Miss Katherine look to such advantage before. If she were more to his taste, he might indeed . . . But amusement threatened to overcome him yet again. 'Come, Miss Katherine,' he said coaxingly, 'you must see that it would not do at all!'

'Really, I can not see that, my lord!' Kate returned stubbornly. 'I think it would answer excellently well. But—I see that you regard it only as a joke, my lord, so I will not waste your time any longer!' And Kate rose, and adjusted her pelisse, all offended dignity.

Lord Barnstaple came up to her swiftly. 'I beg your pardon, ma'am,' he said gravely, successfully suppressing his mirth; 'I have been very rag-mannered. I must thank you for the great honour you have done me in asking me to be your husband, but, with the very greatest regret, I must refuse.'

Kate looked into his lordship's face, suspicious that she would find laughter lurking there. But the earl's face was perfectly serious. Now Kate herself smiled. 'I suppose this is how gentlemen must feel when they have been refused, my lord,' she said wryly.

The earl smiled back into the violet eyes. 'But—your heart is not broken, I think?'

Kate beamed and shook her head. 'No, my lord. My pride, a little, perhaps, but that only a little. But it did seem such a good idea, my lord; and you must admit, if I had not come to you, you would never have thought of me, would you?'

Lord Barnstaple shook his head.

'You see? Well, my lord, it seems a pity that you have turned down a wife who would not have been the least worry to you, my lord, for I meant what I said. After all, when the affections are not engaged, a friendly toleration may make for a very comfortable life.'

It was on the tip of the earl's tongue to remark that he supposed his visitor must have a good deal of experience of such things, but somehow he didn't, and instead took Kate's hand and carried it to his lips. 'I think you are a remarkable young woman, Miss Katherine.'

'Merely practical, my lord.'

When he was alone again, Lord Barnstaple sat down in his chair and went over everything that had been said during the recent interview. He wondered why he had not noticed Miss Katherine Netley before. After all, she was a very unusual young woman. Of course, the whole idea was preposterous, but, as he did need to marry, he could do a lot worse than choose Miss Katherine Netley. And the situation had not changed. He would *have* to find a wife soon.

*   *   *

At first, Lord Barnstaple said nothing to his friend about the extraordinary interview with Lord Netley's daughter. Simon Borrowdale arrived some quarter of an hour after Kate had left him, and they made their way to Knightsbridge to view some horses at

Tattersall's.

They followed that by a round or two at Jackson's pugilistic premises, and then the two repaired to their club. It was there that, after extracting a promise of utter silence, the earl confided what had taken place.

Mr. Borrowdale looked blank at first, and whistled thoughtfully. Then he said, with much the same practicality as Kate herself, 'Well, Dick, it might not be such a bad idea. One sister in place of the other. All the other circumstances are identical.'

'I've always preferred blondes, you know that.'

'From what you have told me Miss Katherine said, you would not be stopped—'

'No, Simon. If—when I marry, I would mean to make a go of it.'

Mr. Borrowdale nodded sagely. 'Well, Dick, if I were you, I'd think about it.'

*　　*　　*

On his return to Cavendish Square the earl did indeed sit down at his desk in the library and make an attempt to draft a letter to Miss Katherine Netley. It proved amazingly difficult, and a good many attempts found their way into his wastepaper basket, but in the end he had produced a draft which almost satisfied him. But he could not bring himself to write a fair copy and send it immediately. He

45

would think about it further before he committed himself. Simon was quite right in that the girl would do as well as any, but still the earl hesitated.

Accordingly, he slipped the draft into one of the desk drawers, and spent a calm, peaceful hour rearranging his most recent acquisitions of porcelain.

CHAPTER FOUR

That evening the two men, after dining at Lady Aston's, decided on the spur of the moment to take in the last act at the opera. They arrived at the theatre a little before the end of the last interval, went directly to the Barnstaple box, and proceeded to quiz the company present. All around them the boxes were in motion as the audience resumed their seats, and the two men acknowledged friends and rose to bow to those ladies who caught their eye.

It was shortly before the lights were dimmed for the last act when a little buzz went through the company. In a box well to the left of his lordship's, a small party entered and took their seats. It consisted of three persons: two gentlemen who were slightly known to the two in the Barnstaple box, namely Lord Rupert Pelly and the Baron Marsfold, both of whom were notorious as rakes and gamesters, and who were not received in the best society, although, because of their family connections, they were known to its members.

The third occupant of the box was a woman dressed in a silk gown of broad stripes of yellow and black, which would have made her immediately noticeable in any case. The fact that the face above the gown was dazzlingly beautiful, and that the glossy black curls were arranged in an Apollo knot with an emerald diadem and Glauvina pins, only added to the effect and confirmed the woman as the cynosure of all eyes.

'Good God, Dick! Do you know who she is?' Simon Borrowdale burst out, his eyes almost starting from his head.

When his companion made no reply, Simon turned to the earl, saying, 'Have you ever seen such a creature! That hair and that milky skin? Where on earth can she have sprung from?' Mr. Borrowdale then became aware that his friend Dick was looking suddenly decidedly pale. The earl's jaw was set, and he was staring at the other box as if he had seen a ghost. Abruptly he gave a stiff, unsmiling bow.

Simon turned to see whom the earl was acknowledging, and saw the captivating creature in the box bowing in their direction. There was a delighted smile on the beauteous woman's face, and she raised her hand in a slight wave. Now she seemed to laugh a little,

47

and spoke quickly to her two companions, who now also bowed to the earl, grinning abominably.

'You know her Dick!' Mr. Borrowdale's voice was almost indignant. 'Where the devil have you been hiding her?'

The house light dimmed then as the candles were extinguished, and the earl took his friend's arm. 'We must go!' he muttered urgently.

'But we have only just come!'

'Nevertheless, we must go! At least, *I* must go! I can not stay here now!'

'Well, of course I will come with you!' Simon whispered, following the earl from the box; 'but, 'pon my soul, Dick, you might explain to a fellow! And I had hoped to have another look at that little ladybird!'

Lord Barnstaple did not pause till they were outside upon the pavement again. He waited impatiently for his coach, desperate to get away from the theatre, and scarcely attending to his friend who was demanding to know where the earl had met the fair one, and why he had not presented Simon to her long ago.

'I tell you, I do not know her, Simon!' Lord Bamstaple said with extreme vehemence as they were driving away from the theatre.

'Not know her! Well, she certainly appears to know you!' Mr. Borrowdale looked accusingly. 'You bowed to her! I saw you! You *must* know her!' When the earl made no reply,

Mr. Borrowdale ventured, 'Do not tell me, Dick, that she left your protection for that Pelly or Marsfold! No wonder you are put out with the creature!'

'She has *not* left me!' the earl cried exasperatedly. Then he said unwillingly, 'I was—acquainted with Marguerite Belleville— years ago. But I do not know her now! And I have no intention of knowing her!'

'Well, I wish you had presented me to her when you had finished with her!'

His lordship made no reply to that, but frowned gloomily.

'Where can she have sprung from!' Simon Borrowdale went on. 'She hardly has the look of having just come up from the country; yet, how is it that she has not been seen before this season?'

'Up from the country!' Lord Barnstaple repeated wrathfully. 'That—that creature is not just—up from the country, Simon! And I warn you, if you get entangled with that—that woman, do not depend upon extricating yourself from her coils with any credit—or with any blunt!'

Mr. Borrowdale looked even more astonished at this outburst. 'It is not like you, Dick,' he protested, 'to be so vehement against any female! I must conclude that somehow she must have injured you. Pray, do explain.'

At first the earl adamantly remained silent, refusing to give the least explanation. But at

49

last, and very grudgingly, he gave a short, highly edited account of what had happened when he was a youth.

Mr. Borrowdale listened in silence till his friend had finished, then said quietly, 'I have never heard the least whiff of this before.'

'That is hardly surprising. I met Marguerite Belleville while I was up at Oxford. You were at Cambridge. My uncle settled the matter, and I went off to Antigua and spent three years managing his sugar plantations there. When I came home in '08, I went almost directly to the Peninsula. Not a word of this must go any farther, mind!'

Simon promised to keep silence, then suggested that they should go to Watiers for the remainder of the evening: a venue that normally produced a feeling of considerable well-being in Lord Barnstaple. But on this particular evening, he could not concentrate upon his cards, with the result that, most unusually, he lost a good deal.

Mr. Borrowdale viewed this outcome with considerable perturbation—not because of the lost money, which the earl could well afford, but as being further proof that his friend was decidedly not himself.

As for the earl, he felt out of charity with the world and himself. On top of the irksome provisions of his uncle's will, to find that Marguerite Belleville was in London was the outside of enough, and he returned to

Cavendish Square and took himself off to his bed in unusually gloomy mood.

But the oblivion of sleep eluded him. He had not thought of Marguerite Belleville for years, and seeing her again so suddenly had been a disagreeable shock. She did not appear to have changed at all: she seemed not one day older. Her beauty had not faded in the least, but it had no power to move him now—except to distaste and irritation.

He wondered uneasily why Marguerite had returned to England: he had always thought that it was part of the agreement that his uncle had made with her that she and her husband should live out of England. Coming on top of his uncle's death, the earl felt that everything was conspiring to cause him harassment, and he felt much injured that the comfortable, carefree life he had enjoyed up to now was falling into ruin.

He wondered where Joseph Belleville was. He had met the man once or twice in the old days: a giant of a fellow, with red hair and a red face and a loud laugh, and a tongue which could charm the birds off the bush. But his wife had told of beatings and unspeakable demands, and Richard, with all the fervour of first love, had wanted only to rescue the lovely creature from such a hateful life.

The shock of finding out that man and wife were in league with each other, and that he was far from being the first young man to have

51

been deceived by the lady, had turned the young Richard Dunthrop into a very bitter person, and had been responsible for him subsequently avoiding any attachment to any member of the fair sex on anything other than a commercial basis.

Seeing Marguerite Belleville again had brought everything unpleasantly to his mind, and the earl spent a very restless, sleepless night.

*   *   *

He breakfasted very late the next morning, feeling positively low. He thought gloomily that it would be just his luck to venture into Bond Street and find himself confronting Mrs. Belleville, which was the thing of all things he most wished to avoid. Even after all the years that had passed, he still felt angry at the deception that had been practised upon him, as well as at the price his uncle had had to pay to save him from an action in the courts by Belleville.

If only he had not written such mawkish letters, had not asked the creature to run away with him. At the time it had seemed romantic, and he had been filled with a chivalrous desire to save his beloved from her dreadful husband. He squirmed as he thought of how he had felt then.

He was reviewing the past, and at the same

time demolishing several boiled eggs and a good-sized piece of chicken pie when a footman came to tell him that there was a lady arrived desirous of speaking to him.

'What name did she give?' the earl asked, almost hoping that it would turn out to be Miss Katherine Netley once more.

'The lady gave no name, my lord, but impressed upon me that I should tell your lordship that it was of the utmost importance that you should receive her.' The footman's voice was non-committal, but his face expressed his disapproval.

His lordship's heart sank into his slippers, but he said, clinging to hope still, 'Did she indeed! Was it the same lady who came yesterday?'

'I do not think so, my lord, for although the lady is veiled, she looked to me a good deal shorter than Miss Netley, my lord.'

Richard's stomach joined his heart, but he got out, quite sharply, 'Pray tell the lady that I am unable to receive her.'

As if to convince himself that his caller would depart compliantly, the earl rose and went to his room, and Jameson began to shave him. The lather was but newly spread upon his chin when the footman appeared again.

'Well, what is it now?' The earl sounded decidedly short.

'The lady asked me to say again, my lord, that it is of the utmost importance that she speak with you. If this morning is not convenient, she will return again at a time to suit your lordship.'

The earl sighed inwardly, but because of the lather, only his eyes betrayed his feelings. Clearly Marguerite Belleville would not let him rest until she had had an interview with him, and he had best get it over now, then give orders that she was never to be permitted to enter his house again.

'Very well. Pray tell the lady that I will be down when I am dressed.'

The man disappeared a second time, and the business of the toilet continued. The earl was silent, and Jameson sensed that conversation was not required, so he went about his work with his usual competence, adjusting the final details of his lordship's appearance in a concerned, sympathetic manner.

Deliberately the earl took his time over choosing a waistcoat: his neckcloth had turned out perfectly at the very first attempt, but he was able to spend several minutes selecting a snuffbox to match his coat.

But at last there was nothing more to be done: the earl was as perfect as good taste, an excellent man and the combined arts of Weston and Hoby could make him. He therefore left his room, and descended the staircase to the library where his visitor awaited him.

As he opened the door, he saw a veiled figure in white by the window near the desk. The morning dress the woman wore was of French lawn, with rather exaggerated gigot sleeves; her head was adorned with a large straw hat on which sat a riot of feathers and flowers and ribbon bows, all of palest cream. A thick veil covered the face.

The figure had been in the act of closing her reticule as the door opened. At the noise, the woman looked up, paused for a moment, then threw back her veil, smiling. In a low, musical voice she said, 'Richard! I knew you would not refuse me! Do you know, my dear—you have not changed one atom—except to have grown more handsome than ever!' And she took a step or two towards the earl and held out a small, gloved hand.

The earl, however, made no move to take it. He merely regarded the woman with an aloof expression, and said in his fashionable, languid manner, 'I did not know that it was you, madam. I confess I am exceedingly surprised to see you. I had thought you settled abroad.'

'And so I was, Richard! So I was! But after all these years I had a yearning to see my native shores again.

'Indeed!'

'Oh, come, Richard, do not be so cold. I know it is many years since we met, but I have most happy memories of our times together.' And the visitor came still closer and smiled beguilingly into the earl's face.

'Then your recollections differ materially from my own, ma'am,' came the cold reply.

The beautiful lips parted in a gentle laugh. 'Oh, my dear! Do not say it was all so very disagreeable! I can remember many, many times when we were very happy together.' Now the woman placed a hand lightly on the earl's arm. 'I had been so looking forward to seeing you, Richard.'

'I had thought never to see you again!' the earl returned indifferently. He regarded her coolly for a moment, then added, 'You told my man that it was of the utmost importance that you speak to me. Pray state your business, ma'am.'

The huge dark eyes looked reproachful now. 'It was not like you to be churlish, Richard! One of your greatest attractions was your perfect manners. I am sorry to see they have lost something with the passing years. Are not you going to offer me a scat? Must I state my business, as you put it, standing?'

'I can not think that there can be any business between us, ma'am. However, pray take a seat and begin.' The earl gestured briefly at a chair. He himself remained standing in front of the fireplace, one negligent hand resting upon the mantleshelf, regarding his visitor impassively.

With a graceful movement, the woman seated herself, re-arranged her veil a little to more becoming folds, and smiled up at the earl once more. 'It has been a long time, Richard.'

'Seventeen years, ma'am.'

'Such exact recollection must mean, I am certain, that you remember perfectly our time together,' came the laughing answer. 'Oh, please, Richard, do you sit down also, and not stand over me like some terrible schoolmaster! I am not used to such censorious looks.'

'I prefer to stand, ma'am.'

The earl's visitor shrugged slightly. 'As you wish, my dear.' She gazed up at him with limpid eyes. 'Pray permit me to say first how very sad I was to hear of your recent bereavement. I heard but a short time ago. I know how much your uncle meant to you.'

The earl's eyes hardened fractionally, but he merely gave a tiny bow.

'It is always sad when one upon whom we have depended for so long is taken from us.' Seeing that the earl remained impassive and cold, the woman proceeded to take a delicate wisp of lace handkerchief from her reticule, and applied it carefully to the corner of her eyes. 'I felt so much for you, my friend. I, too, have known what it is to suffer the loss of a loved one.'

Still the earl said nothing, but gave a barely audible sigh.

His visitor looked again into the earl's face, her expression tragic. 'Oh, Richard, it is not like you to be so hard! It *was* not like you! You were always a creature of the tenderest sensibilities. I am greatly distressed to see you so changed!'

'I must tell you, ma'am, that I have an engagement later this morning. I would be glad if you would proceed with what you have to say as expeditiously as possible.'

'Very well,' the woman answered pitifully, her voice full of tears. 'Though I must say how very hurt I am by your negligent attitude, Richard. I had expected better from an old friend.'

'I do not recollect that we were—*friends*, ma'am.'

The woman smiled wistfully at that. 'No; we were not *friends*, were we, Richard? Always we were something more than that. Something a deal more affectionate . . .'

'As I recollect it, ma'am, we parted in a very different manner.'

'It is true that, at the end, there was some— little misunderstanding between us. I could have wished it otherwise, but—I am afraid your uncle judged me harshly.'

The melting eyes were again turned beseechingly upon the earl's countenance, but the man maintained his cold, indifferent manner. An expression of boredom was permitted to cross his face.

'But, what was I to do, my dear?' the woman continued in appealing tones. 'You know how it was with me. I was at my wits' end—' A gentle smile curved the lips. 'You had tried to be so kind to me, my dear, helping me—such presents as you showered upon me . . .'

Silently the earl recalled the jewels he had given this creature, some of them family jewels which should have been given only to his own wife. He recollected his own foolishness bitterly now. 'As I recollect, ma'am,' he answered icily, 'they were soon disposed of to meet the debts of yourself and Belleville. They can have meant nothing to you. I am surprised that you remember them now.'

'Then you *do* remember—'

'All this is nothing to the point, ma'am. Pray say what you came to say.'

At that, the lady heaved a sigh. 'You are so changed, Richard! I would not have believed . . .' She applied the wisp of lace to her eyes again, and surreptitiously regarded the earl through the gauzy cloth. She judged that no progress would be made upon the line she was currently following. It was time to move forward.

'I will come to the object of my visit, my dear,' she said brokenly. The delicate eyelids drooped for a moment, and the brim of the hat hid part of the beautiful face. Then the shoulders were straightened, and in a brave voice the lovely tones continued, the eyes liquid with appeal, 'I said a moment ago that I too know what it is to lose a loved one. I must tell you, my dear, that I am now alone in the

59

world. Belleville has departed from me.' And the handkerchief was applied to the eyes yet again, with the very greatest care and delicacy.

If Marguerite Belleville had hoped for any sign of sympathy, she was disappointed. The earl merely remarked, 'Indeed, ma'am?' in the same indifferent manner in which he had spoken before.

'It—it is because of this—terrible—loss—that I have decided to return to my own country. I felt the need to be surrounded by familiar sights, familiar customs, old friends . . .' There was a pause while the handkerchief was employed once more. The earl could smell the scent wafting about the room as the tiny scrap of fabric was moved, but he was not in the least deceived. He knew that the tears, if they existed at all, were but crocodile tears.

Marguerite Belleville, seeing that the earl remained obdurate, and had no intention of making any comment upon her words, continued bravely, 'I decided that at last I should take my place in the society of my own country.' The lustrous eyes looked directly at the earl again now, with perhaps a hint of defiance lurking in their depths.

'Indeed!' was all the earl's reply, yet again.

'Yes. I felt that only in such circumstances should I find comfort in my affliction. I was so young when Belleville and I departed these shores. Scarce eighteen, you recall.'

The earl's eyebrows rose sharply at that,

and he looked for a second as if he might contest the lady's assertion. But in the end, he said nothing.

Marguerite hurried on, 'And because of our—difficulties, you recall that we had never been able to play that part in society which should rightfully have been ours. You know that my mother was a peer's daughter, and my dear Belleville should rightfully have inherited a baronetcy and lands in Ireland ...'

The earl shrugged, the merest quarter-inch raising of one immaculate shoulder.

His visitor now raised her head to look at him directly. 'I think now—to play that part.'

'I congratulate you upon your improved circumstances, ma'am,' the earl returned coldly. 'But I fail to see why you have been at such pains to come and apprise me of it.'

'Richard!' The huge dark eyes were reproachful. 'Because you are my best friend here! I had thought you would be glad to hear it!'

Richard regarded the woman with loathing, but his face remained impassive. He murmured only, 'Indeed!' yet again.

'Yes, indeed, Richard!' The beautiful voice had a slight edge to it now. 'And I thought that, being in the position you are, a little notice from you, a few introductions ...'

At last the earl understood what Marguerite Belleville was after, and his face grew hard. 'I recollect, ma'am, that last night you were with two persons who are connected with some of our best families. Doubtless they will be able to provide you with all the introductions you need.'

'Rupert Pelly and Guy Marsfold!' The delicate shoulders were shrugged disdainfully. 'Oh, come, Richard! You know that, sponsored by them, I should have no chance at all of certain doors being opened to me!'

'I do not perfectly understand what you mean, ma'am,' the earl remarked now in a bored voice.

The lovely eyes looked suddenly angry, and there was a tinge of steel in the beautiful voice when it answered, 'I think you know very well what I mean, Richard! I mean that I wish to be received—everywhere.'

'I still do not see why you come to me, ma'am.'

'Because you are the one person I can go to who would be able to ensure it!'

The earl looked down into Marguerite Belleville's countenance, his disdain evident in his eyes. 'I do not think that I shall be able to help you, ma'am.'

'*I* think that you are able to help me very well, Richard! And I mean that you should!' The last was added very softly, but the steel was more evident now.

'Indeed! And how should I help you, ma'am?'

'You will start by procuring me a voucher

for Almack's.'

'Almack's! You shoot quite past the mark there, ma'am! Even if I would, I can not guarantee your entree there.'

'I expect you to do it, Richard!'

The earl let out an irritated sigh. 'I am astonished that you should come to me of all people on this mission, ma'am! I tell you plainly, I would not lift one finger to accomplish what you wish!' And the earl made to pull the bellrope.

'Not so fast, Richard!' his visitor said menacingly; so menacingly that the earl paused, his hand raised. 'Hear me out first!' she went on more softly. 'I think that you will not be so hasty as to dismiss my request then!'

'Well, ma'am?'

'I *ask* you, once again, to help me, Richard!'

'Never!' And the earl's disdain and loathing were plainly shown in his eyes.

'Very well.' The woman proceeded to open her reticule and take from it a sheet of folded paper. She held it out to the earl. 'Pray read this, Richard!'

The earl hesitated for a moment, then reluctantly took the paper. He unfolded it and read the first few words. As he looked, he felt suddenly sick at the stomach. There before his eyes were the familiar, maudlin words which he had poured out as a green youth, in love for the first time. He looked up at the woman sharply, and said through clenched teeth, '*I*

63

had thought my uncle had paid you well for all the letters, ma'am!' For the first time he was quite unable to keep all emotion from his voice.

Now the woman smiled triumphantly. 'Oh, he did, my dear Richard! But—there were so *many* letters! I had thought I had found them all, but—this one—and a few others—somehow escaped my search! And I should not bother to tear it—or to take a taper to it, my dear! It would make no difference!' And she twitched the paper back, and put it in her reticule again.

'You deceived my uncle also, ma'am!' the earl exploded with abhorrence. 'Besides being a loose woman, you are a cheat and a liar! And now, no doubt, you would try blackmail!'

Marguerite Belleville's eyes were hard and angry, but her voice was silky. 'When I came here this morning, my dear Richard, I had expected to let you off lightly. I had meant only to ask you to smooth my way into society, procuring me cards for receptions I would not otherwise receive—little matters like that. But as you have been so very churlish—and now offensive—' And here the look on the woman's face changed to one of deep malignancy, '—I think I deserve some recompense. You said earlier that you were unable to guarantee procuring me vouchers for Almack's.' The voice paused, and the beautiful face smiled sweetly. 'Well, there is one way, Richard, my dear, which I think could not possibly fail.'

'Indeed, ma'am?' the earl grated.

'Yes, Richard.' The woman's face was amused now. She continued with a smile. 'If you were to request them in the name of your wife!'

The earl stared confounded. 'My wife!'

'Yes, Richard; your wife.' A gentle laugh escaped the rosy lips. 'I have a fancy to be an *English* countess. An Italian title is all very well, but—there are so many of them: all the family, as you know. There is not that disadvantage to English titles. And—the Barnstaple title is a very old and—respectable one!'

'I do not understand you, ma'am. Do I collect that you claim an Italian title?'

'Oh, yes, indeed; did not I mention it before? I am the Contessa Snaguingrazzo.'

'I understood that Belleville had but recently died!'

'Oh no! But when Belleville was taken from me, I married the count.'

'And—how long is it since you were widowed, ma'am?'

The countess shrugged. 'I forget exactly. A year—perhaps more.'

'You did not wait long to replace him!'

The woman shrugged indifferently.

'And where is this—Count Snaguingrazzo?'

'He too—has died.'

'You seem careless of your husbands, ma'am!

The countess gave a gurgling little laugh. This faded to a smile and she said softly, 'Come, Richard. I know that you have not forgotten how it was between us! We were so happy together. We may be happy again! You wanted so much to marry me once!' she ended cajolingly.

'That was before I knew you, ma'am! When I thought you had been ill-used by a heartless husband. But what you ask is quite impossible!' The earl glared. 'I would never insult my friends—!'

'Rumour has it that you need to marry, Richard—' The woman said softly, swallowing her anger with an effort.

'That would not make me turn to you, ma'am!' And the earl turned away in disgust.

'Some—small indiscretions of youth—you can not hold them against me now!'

'Small indiscretions of youth!' The earl faced the woman once more.' I do not remember them as small indiscretions, ma'am! Nor of youth!' he finished brutally.

The countess gazed at him, anger blazing in her beautiful eyes. With an effort she controlled her voice. 'I was right when I said that your manners had grown less polished, Richard! You are hardly a gentleman now!'

'Then allow me to tell you plainly,' the earl

66

retorted, 'that I would never consider allying the Barnstaple name with—with a woman like you, ma'am! How can you think it? I know very well whence you came, ma'am! Your father an ostler, and your husband a mountebank! But I see very well how it is, ma'am! You are returned to England because you have heard of the death of my uncle, and you thought to find the same green youth you knew when you left England! Well, I am not the same, ma'am! I have seen and learnt much since then; and I say to you now, do what you will! It will have no influence with me!'

'You always were impetuous, Richard, my dear! But pray think about it. Would you really care to be the laughing-stock of society? Pray imagine the sniggering! The roasting of your friends! You—who pride yourself on your place in society—such a Corinthian as you are—shown to be the author of such sickly, mawkish sentiment! Oh come, Richard! You would not like it in the least, my dear!'

The earl felt decidedly unwell as he heard the countess's words. If his letter was published, he shuddered to think of the ridicule he would have to endure—and the whole story would certainly come out. But even that would be preferable to being tied to this creature for the remainder of his life. That thought was quite unendurable! Far better that he should have accepted Miss Katherine Netley's offer. How he regretted his hastiness

67

now! Still, it might be made to serve.

'As to that,' he managed to get out with a very fair imitation of his old negligence, 'I really do not mind it—in the least, ma'am. As to your other suggestion—I am afraid you are too late.'

'Too late! What do you mean, Richard?' And the countess smiled at him as she might at a little boy trying to get out of a scrape.

'I mean that—I am not at liberty to marry you, ma'am—even if I wished it.' The lie came out as nonchalantly as if it had been the truth.

'Not at liberty!' The countess was frowning now.

The earl bowed concurrence. 'I am already betrothed, ma'am.'

'I do not believe you! This is but a fudge!'

'I assure you, ma'am,' the earl said loftily, 'I am already spoken for.' He thought of Kate Netley again, and remembered the letter he had tried to write to her. Perhaps, if he were to ask her now, she might yet accept him. After all, it had only been yesterday when she put her proposition to him.

'Then you must break it off!' the countess declared.

'That is quite impossible, ma'am!'

'I think not!'

'Only consider, ma'am! Were I to do as you ask, I should most probably have a breach of promise action brought against me! Such a proceeding might well end in *my* being no

68

longer in a position to open doors at all! In fact, they could well be slammed in my own face!'

The earl could not quite repress a smile as he saw the countess considering his last words. She said at last, 'How is it, then, that no-one has heard of your betrothal, Richard? I have heard often enough that you must marry, but not that you have taken any steps towards that end. It must be a very havey-cavey affair for you to keep it secret! You have not your uncle to consider now, you know!'

'Not at all, ma'am,' the earl said loftily; 'it has but just been arranged.'

'As I thought! It is in your head only!'

'On the contrary, ma'am.'

'Then—who is the lady?'

It was then that the earl saw that he had got himself into deeper waters by his unnecessary embroidery. He should have stuck to a simple refusal, and avoided elaborations. 'You can hardly expect me to reveal that before the lady herself has informed her family,' he temporised.

'Oh, fudge, Richard! You are far too proper not to have set all right with the young lady's father first. Besides, you have not the look of an engaged man!'

'I tell you I am!'

'Then tell me the chit's name!'

How the conversation might have gone was to remain unknown, for at that moment the door opened and one of the footmen

69

appeared. The earl felt a wave of relief that he had not given orders that he was not to be disturbed. He looked towards the man and indicated that he should deliver his message.

'One of my lord Netley's men is come, my lord. He has brought a message from Miss Katherine Netley, who asks if by any chance your lordship has come upon a brooch the young lady has mislaid, my lord. She believes she may have dropped it when she was here yesterday.'

'I have not seen any brooch. Have you asked in the servants' hall ?'

'Yes, my lord.'

'Then you had better return a message regretting that the brooch is not here.'

'Very good, my lord.'

The man withdrew, and the earl turned back to the countess who, he saw with surprised relief, was in the act of lowering her veil. Her face was now hidden, but her laugh was malicious. 'Really, Richard! How forward are young English women today! Visiting you in your own home! So different from what I was accustomed to! And now you may ring for your man to show me out. I shall leave you for a while—to think over what I have said.'

The countess rose at that, and smoothed her gloves in what the earl fumingly considered a provokingly smug manner, quite as if she had not the least doubt in the world that she would get her way.

He felt even more vexed when the countess glanced about the room, then said very patronisingly. 'This really is a quite excellent house, Richard. I shall like being its mistress. Solid and old-established. A trifle old-fashioned, perhaps; I dare say your uncle did very little in that line. But I can soon put that to rights. Oh, you must not allow that to worry you in the least, my dear! I shall be careful that it will not disturb you. Besides, as you remember—I have the most excellent taste.'

Luckily the footman entered then in answer to the bell before the earl could make any tart reply. With a little laugh, which Richard found exceedingly irritating, the countess glided from the room.

CHAPTER FIVE

Kate Netley was sitting alone in her room after returning from a protracted shopping expedition in Bond Street. She had not needed to purchase anything in particular, but had thought that it might help to raise her spirits if she bought herself a new bonnet and went to inspect the new silks recently arrived from France.

Sir James Brocket had appeared early in Wimpole Street again, and she had felt that positively she could not remain under the same roof as her perfidious lover. To think of him closeted with her sister Susan in the library or the morning room was too much, and she had hurried out, accompanied by the maid she shared with Susan.

She had come back, having stretched the shopgazing expedition to last as long as she could. Now she stared at her purchases, thinking that the bonnet she had bought did not look near so pretty as it had looked in the shop, and still feeling herself very ill-used. And now, in addition to the wretchedness she felt over the faithless Sir James, she had the misery of remembering her interview with the Earl of Barnstaple the previous day. What a cake she had made of herself! But—it had seemed such a good idea at the time.

These doleful musings were interrupted by the arrival of a maid who came to announce that a Contessa Snaguingrazzo was below and asking to see her.

Kate racked her brains, but could remember no such name. 'Are you sure the countess asked for me, Sarah?'

'Oh, yes, Miss! Most particularly!'

Puzzled, but thinking that she might as well as not receive the Italian lady, Kate smoothed her hair and went down to the small salon where the countess was waiting. She saw an unknown woman, of rather indeterminate age—the caller might be anything from twenty-four to thirty-four, and dressed in the very height of fashion, and with a certain something about her gown which proclaimed not only that it came from a first-rate dressmaker, but also that it was probably made upon the Continent.

Kate curtsied. 'The Contessa Snaguingrazzo?'

The countess, who had thrown back her veil, smiled delightfully, and Kate was at once aware of what an amazingly beautiful woman her visitor was. 'Miss Katherine Netley?' The inflection was thoroughly English, Kate noted as she acknowledged her identity.

'Will not you be seated, countess?'

With a smile and a graceful movement, the countess took the chair Kate indicated. 'You are so kind.'

'Forgive me, countess,' Kate said, seating herself also, 'I greatly regret that I do not recollect where . . .'

'Oh, Miss Netley, pray allow me to explain. We have not, in fact, actually met before. I have been resident in Italy for some years now, and am but newly returned to England.'

'Oh, I see,' Kate said pleasantly, still wondering what the countess could want with her.

'I know it must seem very strange to you that I should call upon you, Miss Katherine, unacquainted as we are, but—I have just come from a very old—very dear friend, who has told me your news; and I was so—very interested—that I could not stop myself from coming at once to—see for myself my old friend's choice!'

By now Kate was completely at sea, and her puzzlement showed in her face. 'I am afraid that I do not comprehend you, ma'am.'

'Oh, my dear! I was told that the news was not public yet, but, as such a very old and close friend, I hope that you will not mind that your fidanzato—confided in me.'

'My fiancé! Oh, I am afraid you must have misunderstood, ma'am! It is my sister Susan who is betrothed!'

'Your sister Susan!'

'Yes, ma'am. To Sir James Brocket. It will be in the Morning Post tomorrow—or the next day.'

'Sir James Brocket! Forgive me, Miss Katherine, but I know nothing of your sister and this Brocket. But the earl himself told me that you and he—'

'The earl, ma'am?'

'Yes, yes; the Earl of Barnstaple,' the countess replied impatiently.

As she heard the name, Kate's perplexity grew. Now she herself frowned, wondering if she could have misunderstood the earl, and that he had accepted her proposition after all. But—no! She had made no mistake. She could remember the earl's words all too clearly.

She glanced at the countess who was watching her narrowly. 'Forgive me, ma'am,' she said quickly, '—but—do I collect that the Earl of Barnstaple told you that he was betrothed to me?'

'He did indeed!' the countess returned promptly, smiling exultantly. 'But—I—collect that it is not true, is it, my dear?' And she looked at the girl shrewdly.

There was something in the way the countess spoke that raised Kate's hackles at once: a slight patronising tone in the voice which irritated the girl unduly. Besides, if Lord Barnstaple had changed his mind, then marriage to him would suit Kate very well still. She had better find out from his lordship exactly what had passed between him and the contessa.

So, instead of telling the countess plainly that she was not betrothed to his lordship, Kate hesitated a moment, then prevaricated. 'You put me in a difficult situation, ma'am.'

As soon as she had uttered the words, Kate was appalled at herself. She had not exactly *told* a lie, it is true, but she had *intentionally* given the wrong impression. Kate shuddered again at herself, and then once more as it dawned on her that the earl must have discussed her forward behaviour with the countess. He *must* have done, or how could the countess know—Really! She had thought better of him! And yet—somehow the countess had received the wrong impression, and so Lord Barnstaple—

'It is very sudden, I think?' the countess said, interrupting Kate's thoughts.

Kate glanced at the countess, coloured, and hung her head.

'I see,' the countess said slowly. 'Naturally, you would not wish to share the excitement by broadcasting your news at the same time as your sister's.'

Again, Kate did not reply.

'You have known Lord Barnstaple for some time, I suppose?' the countess asked now.

'This is my second season, ma'am,' Kate returned, again inferring something less than the truth. But it was not totally a lie. She had met Lord Barnstaple the previous summer upon one or two occasions; but it was only during the first weeks of the present season that she had seen anything of his lordship with any regularity, when he had frequently asked Susan to stand up with him.

'I see,' the countess said now in decidedly annoyed tones. 'Well, Miss Katherine, I can only say that I was amazed to hear the news of your betrothal to the earl—in view of—' She broke off sharply.

'In view of what, ma'am?' Kate asked in no friendly tone.

'In view of his lordship's previous objections to that state.' The countess rose now and pulled down her veil. 'I am so glad to have met you, my dear,' she added in a voice full of insincerity.

Kate pulled the bell for the footman to come to show the countess out. 'It has been my pleasure, ma'am,' Kate said with equal insincerity.

When she was alone again, Kate sat down and wondered whatever had come over her that she had behaved as she had. Although she had not actually *said* anything that was untrue, she had certainly allowed the countess to believe what was not true. But she had allowed her instant dislike of the countess to lead her into a scrape. Still, if anyone taxed her with it, and she had no dependence upon the countess maintaining silence, she would deny everything, saying that the countess had mistaken her meaning.

Still, Kate did wonder what the earl had said to give her late visitor the idea that they were betrothed. Somehow she must find out.

It was that evening that Kate received a letter from the Contessa Snaguingrazzo enclosing another. The countess's note breathed the pity of one deceived woman to another. 'When I first heard the news this morning, I hurried to see you as fast as I could in order to assure myself of the truth or not of what I had just been told. I could scarcely credit it, and yet, when I charged you with it, I saw that it was indeed as I had feared. Oh, my dear Miss Netley, my heart bleeds for you! You do not know to what sort of a man—a monster, rather, I should say, you have attached yourself! I do not blame you for it, for you have been taken in—as I have been myself. I know, all too well how sweetly the earl is able to speak when he chooses—and how cruelly he can cast a woman off when he is tired of her. Doubtless you will find this hard to believe; being young you will be subject still to all the tender hopes and beliefs of youth. Life has not yet touched you with her blighting breath. As you are now, Miss Netley, so was I once! Confident in the goodness of those I trusted in, those I loved. Ah, what a cruel tale I could tell if I would!

'I know what you must be thinking, my dear! What has all this to do with me? Only read the letter I enclose, and you will understand not only what I would save you from, but what I suffer now. Your friend, Marguerite Snaguingrazzo.'

Greatly surprised, Kate opened the sheet which had been enclosed in the same envelope. Glancing through it at first briefly, but then with rapt attention, she saw that it was the first page of a love letter, dated the beginning of that same month. The writing was impassioned, a distraught lover pleading with the woman he loved to take pity on him—in the most intimate language, and Kate felt a modest blush rise to her cheek. She came to the end of the page and turned it, but there was no more of the letter; only a note scrawled in the countess's hand to the effect that this

78

was but a part, and that the whole could be shown to Kate at any time.

As Kate stared down at the missive, she understood why Lord Barnstaple had said that he must be allowed to choose his wife for himself. He had, indeed, already chosen; he was in love with the countess. Kate blushed again as she thought of her visit to Cavendish Square.

Then, with a frown, Kate recalled the countess's words. It could not be doubted that she had been told by Lord Barnstaple that he was betrothed to Kate. But—surely the countess must have misunderstood! It simply did not make sense! Kate determined that somehow she must see Lord Barnstaple again to clear up the puzzle.

*   *   *

After the countess had departed from Cavendish Square, the Earl of Barnstaple felt so ill-at-ease that he was convinced that nothing would restore him so well as a bout or two with Jackson. Accordingly he took himself off to Bond Street, and the physical exertion he there expended did much to improve his spirits. Simon Borrowdale arrived while he was in the ring, and afterwards the two went to their club, and Simon learnt of the earl's interview with the Countess Snaguingrazzo.

'And—and you told her that you were already

affianced?' Simon demanded.

The earl nodded.

'Well, if the lady is as you say she is, you had better get yourself into that situation as soon as possible,' Simon advised. 'Should not you think again of Miss Katherine Netley? You know she is willing.'

'It seems I have no alternative now,' the earl returned gloomily. 'I know Marguerite Belleville. I shall be led the devil of a dance if I do not provide myself with another bride at once.'

And he determined to call upon Miss Netley at the earliest possible opportunity the following day.

When he returned home that evening to change for dinner, he learnt to his surprise that Miss Katherine Netley had called upon him once more. But she had left no message, and the earl could only conjecture the reasons for it. But the message reminded him of the letter he had drafted to the young lady, and he went to his library with the intention of destroying it. He would call upon Miss Netley and propose to her face to face.

He was considerably put out to find the draft gone. He searched in other drawers of the desk, then summoned a servant to ask if it had been seen. The footman went to the servants' hall, and came back with the message that there had been several screwed up pieces of paper in the wastepaper basket that morning, but that nothing on his lordship's desk had been touched.

It was only late that night, when the earl was settling down in his usual chair at Watiers, that he recollected his first sight of Marguerite Snaguingrazzo as he had entered his library. She had been standing near the desk and had been closing her reticule. With an angry and discomfiting certainty, the earl was convinced that the countess had stolen the draft.

He could not think what she would do with it, but he was unsettled enough to lose a considerable sum of money. He left early, impatient for the next morning to arrive when he might take some positive action.

*   *   *

Kate was distinctly relieved when the earl of Barnstaple was announced. It had taken a good deal of courage for her to call at Cavendish Square a second time, and she was thankful not to have to go a third time. But she would have done so, so necessary was it to clear up the mystery. Besides, she felt she owed it to herself to leave him in no doubt that she felt badly-used that he had spoken of her proposal to the countess.

But when the earl was shown in, he looked so harrassed that suddenly Kate was quite sorry for him, and instead of being all offended dignity, Kate received him very graciously, and invited him to be seated, amazed that the countess could have thought the earl such a monster. But then—if he had jilted the lady— But—the letter she had seen hardly seemed to accord with that.

After the first civilities were over, both felt distinctly ill-at-ease. The earl enquired if the lost brooch had been found, and Kate explained its sentimental value as being a relic of her mother. Then both fell silent, each glancing in some considerable embarrassment at the other.

It was Kate who spoke first. She took a deep breath. 'My lord,' she began, 'something— seems to have occurred which I do not in the least understand. Yesterday I received a visit from your friend, the Countess Snaguingrazzo.'

'You received a visit—!' the earl burst out, horrified. 'I assure you, Miss Katherine, the countess is no friend of mine!'

'Oh, but she said—you had told her—I mean—'Kate broke off, highly embarrassed.

'Told her what, ma'am?' the earl prompted.

Kate took a deep breath. 'The countess appeared to think—that we were betrothed, my lord!' she ended firmly.

'Betrothed!'

Kate nodded.

The earl stared at the girl, his mind whirling, wondering what the countess had been about, how she had found out Miss Netley's name. Even if she had taken the draft of the letter, he had merely addressed it to Miss Katherine. 'I do not understand, ma'am!'

'No more do I, my lord! The countess introduced herself to me as a very old, very dear friend of yours, and said that she had come to—to see her old friend's choice!' Kate quoted.

'But—did not you deny it, ma'am?'

Kate could not repress a blush. 'I—did not, my lord. That is—I did not confirm it either. I was so surprised—in view of what you had said the day before, I knew not what to think. I suppose I thought that—that you *might* have changed your mind, and told the countess . . .'

'I assure you I did not, ma'am! How could you think I would—before I had spoken to you!' And the earl sounded very injured.

'But—how else should the countess think us betrothed, my lord?' Kate returned reasonably.

Lord Barnstaple saw that he would have to make a clean breast of everything. 'I did indeed tell the countess that I was betrothed, Miss Katherine, but at no time did I mention your name to her! I swear that!'

'I am glad to hear that, my lord!' Kate said feeling much better. 'But—how can the countess have learnt my name?'

The earl looked as puzzled as his hostess and was about to say so, when a thought struck him. 'I—I believe I may know, ma'am!

'Oh?'

'I—I have reason to believe that—that the countess removed a certain paper from my desk,' the earl said slowly. 'It—it was the draft of a letter to yourself. In it, I named you as Miss Katherine only, but—while the countess was with me, my servant came in to ask if your brooch had been found, and of course your name was mentioned then. With her knowledge of my draft letter . . .'

'I see. That must indeed be it, my lord.' Kate smiled. 'Well, I am very glad that is cleared up. You say, you had a draft of a letter to myself in your desk. May I ask—what it contained?'

'That is the purpose of my visit this morning, Miss Katherine!' Abruptly, the earl stood up, looking agitated. He took a pace or two about the room, then turned to Kate. 'Miss Katherine! There is no way I can see that I may speak except straightforwardly. The day before yesterday you did me the honour of proposing that we should marry. If your offer remains open, I tell you now that I would be the happiest man in the world to accept it!'

Kate stared at the earl, scarcely able to believe her ears. 'But, my lord—the countess—!'

'What of the countess?'

'You—you are in love with her!'

'What can you mean, ma'am?'

'The letter you wrote the countess, my lord—'

'I wrote her no letter!'

'But—she has sent me the first page of it!'

'What!'

The two stared at each other for some moments. Then the earl said very deliberately, 'Am I to understand, ma'am, that the countess has sent you a letter which she claims is from me?'

Kate nodded. 'A love letter, my lord—in which you say you wish to marry her in no uncertain terms. It is but a part, of course, without signature, but it is headed Barnstaple House. She says she may show me the whole at any time.'

Bewildered, and unhappy, the earl said after a moment, 'May I—see the letter, ma'am?'

Kate felt as embarrassed as her visitor, but she drew the missive from her pocket and handed it to the earl.

He read it through swiftly, his jaw tightening as he did so. Then he folded it again and held it out to Kate. 'I did write those words to the countess—but not last May Day, but seventeen years ago,' he said quietly. Swiftly, he outlined what had happened when he had been young.

Kate heard him in silence, then exclaimed, 'So—the countess is trying to—to blackmail you, my lord! I collect she wishes to marry you now!'

Gloomily the earl nodded, and again Kate was filled with a wave of pity for him. 'And—you do not wish to marry her now?'

'I do not! I never shall. Let her do her

worst!'

Kate regarded her visitor for some moments. Then she said, 'I am glad you say that, my lord, for I confess, I did not like the countess. You asked me a moment ago if my proposal was still open. It is, my lord. It would make me very happy if you would consent to be my husband!' she ended smiling.

The earl stared at her, then caught hold of her hands. 'Oh, Miss Katherine! As I said before, you are a very remarkable woman!' He looked at her very earnestly. 'I will try to make you happy, ma'am—even if we have come together in such a ramshackle way!'

'And I, my lord, promise again all that I said before.'

The earl lifted Kate's hands to his lips and kissed them. 'I can not think, ma'am, why I was such a numbskull as not to seize upon your offer at once!'

*　　　*　　　*

It could not be denied that Lord Netley was distinctly taken aback when the earl of Barnstaple presented himself for the second time that week and asked for the hand of yet another of the viscount's daughters. This time the earl spoke fluently, even enthusiastically, without the slightest hesitation, and Lord Netley heard him out politely.

Only when the earl had finished did the

viscount say with mild doubt, 'You do mean, my lord, my *fifth* daughter—Kate?'

'That is so, sir.'

'Forgive me, but—I only wished to be quite certain—in view of your previous request.'

'I collected, from what you said then, my lord, that you would not have any objection to my seeking the hand of one of your remaining daughters?'

'Not in the least, my lord. Not in the least. As long as Kate is content, my lord, I am content.'

The viscount rubbed his hands happily. Two daughters settled in less than a week, and this second match would certainly be considered the match of the season. His sister Letitia would be furious. Really there was nothing to this business of getting girls settled in life. Susan had gone a little slowly, it is true, but things had come out right there. And now Kate . . .

Some mild paternal compunction made the viscount think that he should talk to his daughter alone. It was obvious that Barnstaple could not be in love with the girl, and it would be best if she understood the fact.

Accordingly, Lord Barnstaple retired, and Kate took his place before her father.

'You are sure this match pleases you, my dear?'

'Oh, yes, indeed, sir, I thank you!'

'You are not, I hope, under the

misapprehension that Barnstaple is in love with you, my dear?' He could not mention the earl's so very recent request for Susan, but then, he had better make sure . . .

'Oh, no, sir! I know very well that it is a marriage of convenience for him—as it is for myself, sir!'

The viscount regarded his daughter with a stab of mild disapprobation. It was all very well getting married for purely practical reasons, and Kate had certainly done well for herself— indeed—he wondered how she had brought it off—but it was quite a different thing to say so baldly. Still, Kate had always been a direct girl, and her head was well screwed onto her shoulders.

'Well, my dear—if you are sure it is what you want . . . ?'

'Oh, it is indeed, sir!'

'Well, I wish you every happiness, my dear,' Lord Netley said, and kissed his daughter. Afterwards, he gave a chuckle, and rubbed his hands.

'Sir?'

'I was thinking of your aunt Parton, child. I know she had hopes for her own girl in this quarter.'

Kate grinned back, but merely said, 'You give us your blessing then, sir?'

'Yes, yes; of course I do. So long as it is what you want. Barnstaple I know is not the man to beat you. Nor will he be one to demean your consequence. I wish you every happiness, my dear.'

*   *   *

The news of the engagement of the second Netley girl that week set the tongues of society wagging with a vengeance.

The viscount's sister, Lady Parton, had learnt of it almost at once. She had looked very sour, and had said to her niece, very tartly, 'Well, Miss, I see that you have not wasted any time, though how you have managed to pull it off, I can not think. Susan, now; I could have understood that, for she is a beauty. But you; you are no more than tolerable, Miss!'

'I think his lordship was looking for a *wife*, ma'am, and not a clothes-horse to show off a new gown, ma'am,' Kate returned daringly.

Lady Parton sniffed, and said with some malicious pleasure, 'I do not suppose for one moment that you were his first choice.'

'I really do not know, ma'am. But—can you think that anyone could possibly have turned down his lordship's offer?'

Lady Parton could only glare, and think how much better a countess's coronet would suit her own daughter Marjory than the chit before her. Really, it was very provoking! She ground her teeth and said dismissively. 'Well, it is known everywhere that Barnstaple had to choose a wife soon. I dare say he felt that one addle-pated gosling would do as well as another.'

And Lady Parton swept off to pour her woes into the ear of her particular friend, Mrs. Arbuthnot, with the result that, when Kate and Lord Barnstaple appeared at the rout in aid of the Fruits of Fallen Women at Lady Thraxted's house off Hanover Square that evening, they excited even more comment and felicitations than had Susan Netley and Sir James Brocket.

Lord Barnstaple had to endure with as good a grace as he could the arch smiles of many matrons, and his shoulder was tapped so often by their fans that it ended up quite sore.

'Oh, you sly creature, you!' one after another gushed. 'To keep it all so close! Making out you were such a misogynist, when all the time you were as susceptible as any other gentleman to a pair of bright eyes!'

And Kate herself had to stand and receive the congratulations of Sir James Brocket himself, which she did, she thought, with exceedingly good grace, not once permitting herself one reproachful look at the perfidious Sir James.

Kate had early noticed the Countess Snaguingrazzo, but had avoided her, as the countess herself had seemed to avoid Kate. But she was not surprised to see that lady come up to Lord Barnstaple when he was a little separated from his betrothed. The countess was dressed in a gown of crimson silk, ruched at the hem and sewn with diamonds; more diamonds glittered in the ravenswing hair, and Kate was impressed, in spite of herself, by the surpassing beauty of the woman. She saw the countess smile into the earl's face, and had to struggle to believe that the earl could not be touched. She then saw them walking away from the ballroom together, but was approached then by a knot of her greatest friends, and had to attempt to answer their questions: how long Lord Barnstaple had been paying his addresses, how he had actually proposed, and a thousand more such matters of such supreme interest to them.

Not unnaturally, Kate found some difficulty in answering some of these questions. After all, she could hardly tell her friends that she had actually done the proposing herself, and she had to make up a good many tender episodes which the earl would have been startled to have had imputed to him.

But all the while, she could not help wondering where the earl and the countess were, and what they were saying to each other. They did not even return to the ballroom when the music started, and Kate felt a little injured. The earl had said he positively did not care for the countess, but—it was too bad for him to abandon *herself* on the very evening of their engagement, and she saw sometimes pity, sometimes triumph in the eyes of those who asked her where the earl was. He was ever thus, they seemed to say. He cared for no woman, and this engagement would not make him change his spots. Miss Katherine Netley might feel that she had pulled off a coup, but in reality, she had not such a very good bargain.

But it was her aunt, Lady Parton, who really put in the dagger. 'What! Not dancing, Katherine! And tonight of all nights! Where is Barnstaple pray?'

'He is gone about a matter of business, aunt. He will not be long, I think.'

'I saw him earlier with that Italian creature—the beautiful countess, I forget her name. I believe that they are *old* friends. He knew her years ago, I collect.' And Lady Parton smiled maliciously at her niece.

'So I understand, ma'am,' Kate returned nonchalantly. 'I have met the lady, and am well aware that she is an old friend of his lordship.'

Lady Parton looked at her niece shrewdly for some moments. Then she leant towards the girl, and said in a confidential whisper, 'Let me give you some advice, my dear. I should not let Barnstaple keep up too closely with *all* his old friends; it never does, you know. They always resent a new wife—because she must come first, of course, where often they have been used to being first themselves.' Here Lady Parton looked meaningly at her niece. 'I am sure you understand me, my dear!'

Kate drew back, shocked and disgusted. It was perfectly plain what her aunt was insinuating: that Lord Barnstaple and the countess had been something *more* than friends. The girl regarded her aunt scornfully. 'Oh, yes, I understand you, ma'am. But I assure you, there is no need for you to feel any anxiety upon my account. Lord Barnstaple and I have a perfect understanding upon the matter. And now, if you will excuse me, ma'am—' And Kate curtsied and swept off from her aunt.

But as she moved, her heart beat more quickly than usual—with chagrin, but also with a myriad other feelings which Kate did not wholly understand. Uppermost was the idea that what Lady Parton had said might be true, and that the earl and the countess might even now be renewing their old intimacy; the girl recalled well enough what she had said about not worrying the earl by enquiring too narrowly into what he did and with whom he did it; but, this evening, at least, she would have expected him to remain by her side.

That the earl had shown open animosity towards the countess Kate quite forgot as she sped across the floor intent on avoiding further pitying glances. She hurried from the ballroom, and began looking for her betrothed and the countess in the sitting-out rooms. There were a great many of these, for Lady

Thraxted's house was very rambling, and it took her quite some time to investigate them all.

However, after some more than ten minutes' search she had just placed her hand upon the handle of one door when she heard voices within, and paused. To hear more clearly, Kate put her head closer to the wood, and was not surprised, but was certainly shocked, to hear the countess say, 'I tell you, Richard, it must be broken off!'

And Lord Barnstaple's voice came in reply, 'And what, pray, shall be my excuse?'

Kate's feelings at that were more than outraged; she was plunged into the dismals also. She scarcely heard what the countess said next for the sudden thumping of her own heart, and the choke in her throat which took her breath away.

But she heard Lord Barnstaple's next speech plainly enough. 'I ask you, again, madam, how you expect me to emerge from this with any credit? Of course what you ask is impossible.'

'Oh, I think not, Richard, my dear,' Kate heard the countess answer, very softly.

Kate could bear no more. Resolutely she grasped the handle of the door firmly, turned it and flung the door open. She saw the countess leaning close to the earl, her hand upon his arm, smiling up into his face. At the sound of the door opening, the earl and the countess both turned.

The countess's smile grew broader. 'Ah, Miss Katherine herself! How very timely. Now you may tell her, Richard!'

CHAPTER SIX

When the countess had first come up to him, Richard had had no intention of getting inveighed into a tête-à-tête with her. Indeed, that was the very last thing he wanted, and he was thankful that others were also surrounding him, offering their good wishes for his future happiness. That some of these were patently insincere did not worry him in the least; he knew that some ladies must be chagrined, and feel not unnaturally that Lord Netley, being a man, and having got off two girls in half a week, must have some secret of which they were unaware, but which should be solely female property.

But somehow these others faded away, till only the countess was left. She lost no time then in making her displeasure known, berating him for having announced his betrothal, and demanding that he should make it plain immediately that a mistake had been made, and that he was not engaged to Miss Katherine Netley, but to herself.

Richard became aware that several persons

95

had begun to eye them with some curiosity, and felt that it would be far better to escape the importunate countess, and had accordingly made plain his intention of so doing. But the countess was not to be shaken off, and very angry now, Richard had said coldly that it would be better not to wash their dirty linen so publicly, but to repair to some quiet room till the countess had had her say.

He had been alone with the countess for some little time. The lady had grown increasingly angry, demanding that he make an announcement at once to the effect that he was not betrothed to Miss Netley, and Richard saying as forcibly that such a proceeding would make sure that every door of consequence would be shut against him, and therefore against her also, when the door opened and Miss Katherine appeared in the doorway, her face a little flushed, but otherwise looking perfectly calm and collected.

What Richard's own feelings were at that moment, he was not quite sure. Some relief that his uncomfortable interview had been interrupted, but more dismay that it had been his betrothed who had made the interruption. He gazed at her for a moment, overcoming his surprise, watching her with some fascination, for she looked absolutely cool, and not in the least taken aback by the situation in which she found him.

The girl smiled at him, and then looked

enquiringly at the countess. 'And what, pray, ma'am, should—er—Richard—tell me?' She stressed his name very slightly.

The countess turned to Richard. She waited for a moment, and when he did not speak, she prompted, 'This is an excellent time, Richard; pray do not waste it.'

The tone of the countess's voice grated on Richard's car; its assumption that he would do as she wished was enough to make any man rebel; now as he gazed from the countess to Kate Netley he thought that there was no choice to be made as to which woman he would prefer to be married to: Kate might not be so beautiful, but she was by far the more agreeable creature.

He said shortly, 'I have no intention of saying anything to Miss Katherine . . .' He saw the countess's lips curl sarcastically, and added, '. . . of the matter about which we have been speaking.'

'No?' The countess said silkily; 'then I shall have to tell the young lady myself.'

'I would not advise that, madam!' Richard said coldly.

'I daresay not, my dear Richard! Nevertheless, I intend to do so!' And the countess turned to Kate with a rather satisfied smile upon her countenance.

'Well, madam,' Kate said pleasantly, 'and what is it you have to tell me that my betrothed finds so difficult?' She smiled indulgently, as though she and the countess were two mothers discussing the antics of their small boys.

Richard, through clenched teeth, said quickly, 'I forbid you to speak, madam!'

'You are in no position to forbid or not to forbid, my dear,' the countess remarked, then turned back to Kate. 'It is merely this, Miss Katherine. You called Richard your betrothed a moment or two ago; he can not be that, for I must tell you, that he is engaged to me.'

Kate's expression showed very little emotion; Richard could not but admire the way in which she maintained her composure, for surely this must come as an abominable surprise to her. 'Indeed, ma'am!' the girl said, in just the same voice as she might have used if she had been told that it had suddenly started to rain. But then, Richard thought, she had no attachment to him, so perhaps it was not surprising. Now she turned to him. 'Is this so, Richard?'

'It most certainly is not!'

Kate turned back to the countess. 'In view of what Richard says, ma'am, I must take leave to doubt your claim.'

'Of course, I should expect you to say that,' the countess replied nonchalantly, 'but—I would remind you of the letter I sent you.'

'Ah, yes, the letter.' Kate regarded the countess coolly. 'I asked his lordship about that, and he told me that he had indeed

98

written such a letter to you—but years ago.'

The countess laughed. 'Certainly, Richard has always had a tendre for me, my dear, and certainly—he did write me many letters years ago. But—I assure you, he has not changed.' And the countess looked fixedly at Kate.

'I must beg leave to doubt that, madam,' Kate said equably. 'Since making his professions to you—if indeed he did—Lord Barnstaple has clearly changed his mind. He is now betrothed to me.'

'But—I have rights! And I intend to protect them!'

'With such an old letter, madam?'

The countess made no answer but smiled as if she held a great secret.

'And—pray what do you propose to do, madam?' Kate went on.

'Nothing—if Richard does as I ask.'

'I'm damned if I will!' Richard cried now.

But the countess continued to smile blandly, and did not flick so much as one glance at him.

'And—what do you wish him to do?' Kate asked still equably.

'Make a public announcement that a mistake has been made, and that he is betrothed not to you but to myself.'

'Are you in love with Lord Barnstaple then, madam?' Kate asked simply.

The countess gave a delighted laugh. 'I—have a fancy to be the Countess of Barnstaple.'

'But—I do not understand you, madam!

You have such a title already!'

'An Italian one. And, the English being what they are, they are not all ready to receive it.'

'I see. You wish, I collect, to enter English society.'

The countess smiled her acknowledgement.

Kate turned to Richard. 'Well then, my lord, surely you may present the countess where she would wish to go, without going to the lengths of marrying her?'

'I am not going to marry her!' the man ground out.

The countess spoke quickly, as if the earl had not said a word. 'Oh, no, Miss Katherine, that will not do! That was, I admit, my first thought; but—I wish for rather more now. I wish to have an unassailable place in Society, and as the Countess of Barnstaple I should have such a place. Besides, I collect that Richard must marry very shortly. It seems to me an admirable arrangement.'

Kate nodded as if in agreement, then she said, smiling, 'There is, however, one small difficulty, ma'am.'

'And what is that, my dear?'

'The earl of Barnstaple is betrothed to myself, and so it has been announced to all the world.'

'Then that betrothal must, as I have said before, be broken off.' The countess spoke equally sweetly, reasonably.

'And—if I do not agree to the rupture, ma'am—?'

'If it is not broken off,' the countess said deliberately, 'then I should have no option but to sue Richard for breach of promise!'

Richard heard this and looked, as he felt, appalled. He had stupidly not thought of this outcome before. Always the most unpleasant of lawsuits, mud invariably stuck to even the most innocent of parties. He shuddered to think of his private life being made a public spectacle.

Kate now said, with every sign of composure, 'But surely, you must see that, even if successful, that must ensure that many doors would be permanently closed to you?'

The countess shrugged.

'Your real aim, then,' Kate continued, 'is to ruin Lord Barnstaple?'

'No. I would much prefer to be the countess. But, if Richard is obdurate . . .'

Kate regarded the countess quietly for a moment, then turned to Richard. 'What would you wish to do, my lord? I see it is not an easy choice, but I shall quite understand if you now choose to break off our—'

'I do not!' Richard burst out. 'I will not!' He felt as if he were in a nightmare, and that he must wake soon. Such things did not happen in his well-regulated life.

'Think well, my lord,' Kate said gravely. 'If you do not, you will assuredly be dragged through the courts, the centre of a shocking scandal.'

'I do not care!' Richard cried rather wildly. 'I will *not* marry that woman!'

'You seem to forget, my lord,' the countess now said sweetly, 'that if I do bring such an action, Miss Katherine's name can not be kept out of it!'

Now Richard turned to Kate, his face a mask of misery. 'I had not thought—' he began, then turned to the countess. 'Do what you will with me, but—leave Miss Katherine alone!' he cried.

'My dear Richard, how could I? She is at the centre—'

'No! I am at the centre! I refuse to marry you! It is nothing to do with Miss Katherine!'

'I feel certain people would believe that she had alienated your affections from me! How could she be uninvolved?'

Richard's shoulders slumped then, and he felt himself a beaten man. 'In that case, I must do as you ask,' he said dully.

The countess smiled triumphantly. 'You are very sensible, my dear. It is quite the best thing to do.'

Richard's defeated look had moved Kate to the quick. She had never liked—never trusted the countess. Suddenly she was swept by a determination that the odious woman should not have her way! She, Kate Netley, would save Lord Barnstaple—not because she was the least in love with him, but because she would not allow this creature to cheat him into marriage with her!

Now she said in a musing voice, 'Of course, if *I* were to sue his lordship for breach of promise, then you would have very little chance of entering society, ma'am, as the countess of Barnstaple—or anything else.'

Richard turned to Kate amazed and now injured. 'You also, ma'am!' He was surrounded, it seemed, by intrigue and the threat of open scandal, which he had done nothing to deserve.

As for the countess she stared at Kate for a moment, clearly taken aback, then said quickly, 'You forget, it is *I* who have the prior claim!'

'But it is *I* who am known publicly to be betrothed to his lordship!'

Richard stared from one woman to the other, his mind almost numb. He had expected nothing but evil from the countess, but—that Kate Netley should threaten him also! Whatever way he turned now, this would certainly be the scandal of the season, if not the decade. Possibly even of the century! Richard's gloomy thoughts proliferated with distressing fecundity.

'I shall bring an action at once!' the countess cried.

'Pray do so, ma'am, and that will be your only joy. For I promise you, if you do, you will at once have every door of consequence in society closed against you! I shall see to that!'

'You!'

'Yes, madam, I! My father is connected with most of our first English families. My mother also. My eldest sister is married to the heir to the marquis of Wiltshire; my second sister is married to Lord Frankland. I have two more sisters, ma'am, one married, one about to be married. My aunt is Lady Parton, and the duke of Wellington is my godfather!' And Kate stared at the countess with a triumphant glint in her eye.

Richard felt like uttering 'Bravo!' for he could not help but admire Kate's tirade, but he felt too put out to do other than glare from one woman to the other.

The countess surveyed Kate angrily for some moments, then said with an obvious effort to be calm, 'It seems, Miss Katherine, that we shall have to affect a compromise.'

'A compromise, ma'am?'

'Yes. it is plain that whichever of us Richard chooses, the other—'

'I have already made my choice!' Richard burst out. 'But if this goes on, then I may well marry neither of you!'

'In that case, you will certainly have to face two actions for breach of promise,' the countess remarked dismissively, and turned back to Kate. 'Now Miss Katherine, it is plain that only one of us may marry Richard.'

'I shall never marry you!' Richard reiterated.

'—And I do not mean to withdraw,' the countess continued as if the earl had not spoken.

'Neither do I, ma'am!'

'But—if you love Richard, surely you would wish to save him from such public contempt as must inevitably fall on him if I bring an action?'

Kate appeared to think for a moment. 'You are in the right, ma'am,' she said at last.

'What I propose, then, is that you should announce that you have changed your mind.'

'And you would not bring an action?'

'Not if Richard agreed to marry me.'

Kate turned to the earl. 'It seems that you must agree, my lord, if you are to escape public ridicule.'

'I will not—'

'Be silent, Richard. You grow tedious!' the countess snapped.

'It seems, my lord, that I must break our engagement,' Kate said slowly. 'I could not bear to see you exposed to—to what must happen.'

There was something in the way the girl spoke that convinced the earl that she was genuine. His previous indignation against her melted away as though it had never been. He stepped forward and caught hold of her hands, 'I will not release you, Miss Katherine—'

'Only think, my lord, I beg you!'

Stricken, the earl gazed into her eyes, and knew again that he could not drag this girl's name through the courts. 'Very well,' he said quietly, 'I will agree to whatever you decide.'

Kate smiled at the earl, then withdrew her hands and turned to the countess.

'I shall break the engagement at the end of the season. That will give some credibility to the idea that I have found his lordship and I are not really suited after all. I have no wish to be given the name of a jilt, and I shall need that time.' And Kate smiled at the countess as though they were discussing the arrangements for some reception.

'Ah, but my dear Miss Katherine,' the countess said with a smile, 'there is one little difficulty. I am not prepared to wait so long.'

'But I am not prepared to break off the engagement in less!' Kate smiled equally sweetly.

'I have a notion to be presented this season. And to dance the waltz at Almack's this season also.' And the countess's dark eyes glittered.

'And—I would remind you that I am not quite powerless,' Kate returned meaningly.

The countess gave her a baleful look, and said after a moment's thought. 'Very well. I suggest another compromise. You will break off your betrothal at the end of June. That will give you time enough for you to discover that you and Richard are incompatible.'

'The end of June,' Kate pondered. 'Very

well, ma'am, I accept.'

'And—it is agreed that you will bring no action, nor do anything to hinder my entry into society?'

'As you will agree to return any letters of his lordship's that you may retain, nor will you mention to anyone this arrangement? Of course, if at the end of that time you decide that you do not wish to be the countess of Barnstaple—'

'There is no likelihood of that, my dear Miss Katherine!' The countess smiled at Kate and at Richard. 'I shall leave you now, so that you may begin to get to know each other a little better, and find you do not agree so well together in spite of everything. There is no point in wasting time, is there?'

And with her usual gentle laugh and parting wave, the countess glided from the room.

Kate and Richard stared at each other for some moments when they were alone. Then Richard said slowly, 'Were it not for the thought of dragging your name through the courts, I should never have agreed.'

'I know,' Kate said gently. 'And were it not to save you from the same fate, *I* should not have agreed.' She smiled into Richard's face and a slight blush rose in her cheeks. 'But—we needed the time, my lord.'

'The time?'

Kate nodded. 'I had to buy as much as I could. We have—what is it now—some six weeks till the end of next month. A little less, perhaps.'

'I still do not understand you, Miss Katherine.'

Kate looked at him impishly. 'You may call me Kate, my lord—since we are betrothed!'

Richard felt himself suddenly overwhelmed by some emotion he did not understand. All he could do was take hold of Kate's hand and press it to his lips.

Kate looked down at the bent head, her hand lying still for a moment; then she drew it back and said practically. 'We must not waste time, my lord. We must think—as we have never thought before!'

'Still I do not understand you—Kate.'

'We have till the end of June to find some way to foil that detestable woman!'

'You mean—you were not speaking the truth when you told her that our betrothal would be ended at the end of June?'

'I shall do that, my lord, only if it the only way to save you from a most disagreeable scandal.'

'But—Kate—why do you do this for me? I mean—ours was but a—a business arrangement!'

Kate looked at Richard, an odd little smile upon her lips. 'Let us just say, my lord, that I do not care to be bested by a woman like the countess. She aroused my will to fight, my lord. I did not see why she should have everything her own way—without a fight. And—because I love justice, my lord. And what the countess would do is not just!'

Richard would have given a good deal to take Kate's hand again—to express to her what he felt—for her courage.

But she kept her distance from him. Now she said impersonally, 'Let us review the matter, my lord. The countess holds a letter— or letters you wrote to her years ago, and would claim that they are recent. Even if it could be proved that they are as old as you say—they may even be forgeries, of course, the action she would bring would be exceedingly distasteful—'

'And one which I would give everything to save you from, Kate!'

Kate smiled briefly—'if you did not marry her. I can threaten a counter-action, but the countess is not to know that I would never dream of bringing it.' Kate looked at Richard piercingly. 'The countess is very beautiful, my lord,' she said softly, her voice a little wistful.

'In appearance only!'

Kate smiled again as if satisfied. 'Now, my lord, we must decide what may be done.'

'But—what can be done?'

'There are some possibilities, my lord—'

'That we should *steal* the letters, you mean?'

Kate shook her head. 'I do not think that would be the least use, my lord. I suspect that always there would be more—sufficient to enable her to bring a case against you. No, my lord. I was thinking of something quite different.'

'And that is—'

'We must find something to the countess's discredit—'

'Blackmail, you mean!' Richard demanded, somewhat shocked.

'And what weapon does the countess use against you, my lord?' Kate demanded reasonably. 'Have not you heard, my lord, that you must fight fire with fire?'

'I can not like it!' Richard said quietly.

'No-one can like it, my lord! But—why should that creature come and upset us all? Why should you be forced to a lifetime's misery with her? Would you wish to be exposed to scandal, my lord? No! Of course not! Oh! I see not the least harm in fighting back!'

Richard smiled admiringly. 'Wellington could have made good use of you in the Peninsula!'

'He is my godfather, my lord!' Kate said proudly. Then, in a very determined voice, she continued, 'Do you know anything we might use against the countess, my lord?'

Richard shook his head. 'I know how she tricked me in the past. I know that the letter must be a forgery, or that she deceived my uncle when she said that she had returned all my letters.'

'Something else, my lord! That is no use to us. It is merely your word against her own.'

The earl shook his head again.

'Well, I am convinced there must be something! What of those others you said had been deceived by the countess?' The earl shook his head. 'In that case,' Kate continued, 'as the countess has been abroad these last years, we are most likely to find what we are seeking on the continent. Have you a friend, my lord, upon whom you may depend utterly?'

Mentally Richard scanned a list of his friends. He had many such, of course, but upon how many could he depend 'utterly'? There was only one name that sprang to mind at once. 'I would trust Simon Borrowdale with my life,' he said at last.

'Would he put himself out very materially for you, my lord? I do not mean something so little time-consuming as acting as your second in a duel, or anything of that kind!'

'I would trust Simon, Kate!'

'He knows of the countess's designs?'

Richard nodded.

'Would he go to Italy for you, my lord, to make enquiries there?'

'But I must do that!'

Kate shook her head. 'No my lord. If you were to disappear from London, the countess would suspect at once—she might even guess correctly what was afoot, and take action

111

immediately. You must see that it must be someone else, my lord.'

* * *

The earl continued to demur, but in the end came to see Kate's point of view, and together they went in search of Mr. Borrowdale.

CHAPTER SEVEN

As Kate left the room with the earl, she wondered very much if she had done the right thing: if she had not, in fact, merely delayed the moment when she would have to withdraw from her engagement with Lord Barnstaple. For, withdraw she most certainly would, and leave the way clear for the countess, if it meant that his lordship could avoid a most disagreeable scandal. It was no part of Kate's plan to injure his lordship.

However, she did not mean to give up without a fight.

In the ballroom she looked eagerly about for Mr. Borrowdale, not even feeling the least tinge of misery as she saw Sir James Brocket dancing with Susan.

As luck would have it, Mr. Borrowdale was not dancing, but caught sight of them at once, and made his way over to them. 'Miss

Katherine! Dick! Is this true? I have just been told—'

'Oh, yes, it is true enough—'

Then, of course, Mr. Borrowdale must offer them his own felicitations. 'Dick! This is excellent news! I am so very pleased—Miss Katherine! I am delighted—'

Kate was pleased that Lord Barnstaple's best friend should so clearly approve. She had known Mr. Borrowdale since the last season, but did not know him well. Now she regarded him more carefully than ever before. She liked his frank, open look, and his honest eyes. He was a friend, she felt, upon whom the earl could well depend. Her spirits rose.

The three slipped away to one of the sitting-out rooms, and between them Kate and the earl explained what they wanted of him.

Mr. Borrowdale was ready to leave at once. 'I will ride to Dover tonight, Dick: I may even catch tonight's packet. And believe me, if there is anything to be found to the discredit of the Countess Snaguingrazzo, whether it be in Florence, or anywhere else, I shall find it!'

The earl gripped his friend's hand in gratitude, and Kate began to feel even hopeful.

The two men departed to arrange Mr. Borrowdale's journey, and Kate returned to the ballroom, filled with excitement. God willing, Mr. Borrowdale would be successful, and they would rout the countess completely!

She was jerked back to earth by hearing her aunt Parton's voice addressing her. 'What, Katherine?' that matron said maliciously; 'still without Barnstaple? Abandoned again? Really, my dear, if I were you, I should insist that I had a little more of his lordship's attention. I have not seen you stand up with him once, and if you do not command his attention in the earliest days of your betrothal, how can you expect it when all the newness of marriage is worn away, and you settle down into a humdrum life?'

' 'Pon my soul, ma'am, I have no wish to be in his lordship's pocket—nor he in mine. And I must say, you quite put me off the idea of marriage if the dreariness you mention is all I may expect! It hardly seems worth making the effort to catch a husband at all. And yet I see all around me females doing little else. I hope my cousin Marjory is enjoying the ball?' Kate ended with a kind smile.

'Thank you. Your cousin has not been without a partner for one single dance,' Lady Parton said crossly, and moved on.

She was next approached by her sister and Sir James Brocket. 'What has become of Barnstaple, Kate?' Susan demanded. 'I have not seen you stand up once with him yet.'

'There is some business that he must attend to, that is all.'

'Well, I can not have my future sister-in-law a wallflower all evening!' Sir James now said roundly. 'May I hope that you will stand up with me next—Kate?' And he smiled that same smile that had been always used to turn her knees to jelly.

But now she protested, not in the least wanting to dance with him, 'There really is no need, sir; I do not mind in the least!'

'But I do!' Sir James answered.

And Susan was happy to add her own urgings.

So Kate found herself standing up with the man she had been in love with for the best part of two seasons. But his gallant look quite failed to move her now. Her mind was totally occupied with wondering what Lord Barnstaple and Mr. Borrowdale were now doing, and how soon arrangements could be made for the latter to start upon his journey, and she hardly heard what Sir James said to her.

It was only later that she thought how curious it was that Sir James had had so little effect upon her.

*　　　*　　　*

The days began to speed by with alarming swiftness. Every day Kate was with Lord Barnstaple, and when they were alone together, there was no other subject of conversation between them but speculation as to where Mr. Borrowdale now was, and what he might have found out about the countess.

The day the letter arrived announcing that he had crossed the Italian border brought broad smiles to both their faces.

'It can not be long now, my lord!' Kate breathed excitedly.

'No! Simon should reach Florence by tomorrow at the latest. He may even be there now!' Richard had been infected by Kate's enthusiasm, and now was as hopeful as she that Simon would find out something which would confound the countess.

'And—he will go directly to the Police Commissioner—and, if he writes that evening—we may hear within—five days, my lord!' Kate cried, counting off the days on her fingers.

'If there is anything to be discovered,' Lord Barnstaple added soberly.

'Oh, but there must be, my lord! There must be! I am convinced of it!'

The earl only looked as if he would give everything he had for that to be true.

There came a further letter from Mr. Borrowdale, when he reached Genoa.

But after that, there was silence.

Each morning the earl called upon Kate in Wimpole Street, and each morning his grave face told her the news before he had uttered a word.

'I fear greatly for Simon's safety, Kate,' Richard said when nearly a fortnight had gone by and there was still no word from Simon Borrowdale.

Kate nodded, her own face worried. Then she forced herself to look cheerfully. 'You must remember that you bade him not waste time writing, my lord, until he had good news. And—we have ample time yet till the end of the month. We must not despair.'

'He had to pass through a country full of bandits. Who knows what may have befallen him?' Richard sounded more than usually worried. 'Oh! I should have gone myself! I had no business to let Simon depart upon what should have been my errand!'

'But Mr. Borrowdale was only too happy to go, my lord!' Kate cried rousingly. 'Besides, you know we thought it best that you should remain here! Apart from anything else, it would have looked very odd if you had left me so soon after our betrothal.'

'I know, Kate—but—if anything should happen to Simon, I could not forgive myself!'

'You must not permit yourself to worry, my lord! There are a hundred things which might have happened which are not of the least consequence.'

'Or which are!' the earl returned gloomily.

Kate set her mind to cheering the earl, pointing out to him a dozen different reasons why he should have received no letter from his friend. But to herself she did admit that she would have been very glad to have had definite

117

news of Mr. Borrowdale.

*   *   *

As for that gentleman, up to the time of his reaching Genoa, everything had gone as smoothly as possible. Not one cast shoe, not one lame horse; not even one inn-keeper who had attempted to overcharge him. He was travelling alone, having brought no servant with him, in order to move as expeditiously as possible, and when he reached Genoa, he sent a brief note to his friend to apprise him of the fact, and bidding him not despair and give way to the countess.

He had no sooner written the note and left it at the post, than disaster struck. He was crossing the street, making his way back to his hotel for a well-earned meal, when one of the mangy curs with which the great port was plagued attempted to seize some flyblown titbit from under the hooves of a carriage horse. The horse took fright, reared, and then set off at a gallop over the cobbles. It careered round a corner, dragging its chariot bumping behind it, just as Simon was crossing the road. He stepped back quickly to avoid being knocked down by it, and in so doing slipped upon some piece of decaying vegetation, and fell, putting out his arm instinctively as he went down.

The result was that he fell heavily on the

118

arm, and he heard a sharp click, and the jolting bruising he received as he touched the ground were all overwhelmed by a terrible pain in his right arm. For a moment, he felt quite sick, and sat in the roadway, trying to gather his wits.

In less than a moment, a hoard of humanity was pressing round him, reeking of dirt and garlic, and all shouting at the tops of their voices as to what should be done, how the accident had occurred, who was responsible and where Simon should be taken.

Luckily for Simon there was one fellow, better dressed than the rest, who stepped forward and began feeling his legs and arms. It was only a second before he discovered what was wrong, and Simon winced as the man took a great coloured handkerchief from his pocket, made it into a sling to support the broken arm, and gave some orders which resulted in a sedan chair materialising, into which the man helped Simon, and then walked beside him till they reached a heavy wooden door, where the chair stopped; the stranger helped Simon out, and into a house which was well furnished in a middling sort of way.

By this time, however, Simon's arm had begun to throb, and he was past noticing details about him. The man seated Simon in a chair, removed the sling, and proceeded to examine the broken arm thoroughly. Simon gritted his teeth while this was happening.

119

When the man reached his shoulder, Simon felt a sudden stab of searing pain, and passed out.

*   *   *

When he came to himself again, he found he was lying in bed, attired in a strange nightgown, his arm bandaged close to his chest. As Simon opened his eyes, a figure jumped up from the chair near his bed, and went to the door and shouted,

'Signore! Signore!'

In a moment, the man who had helped Simon from the street entered the room, and smiling, let out a flood of Italian.

With an effort, Simon gathered his wits together, and attempted to answer in that language.

'Ah, you are English!' the man exclaimed in very passable accents. 'Allow me to present myself. I am Alfredo Motta, a surgeon here in Genova. I am afraid your arm in broken.'

Simon smiled weakly. 'I thought as much.'

'But I have set it,' Signor Motta went on. 'It will be how do you say—as good as new. You will stay here for three weeks—four weeks, and I promise you, it will be—'

Simon attempted to sit up. 'Three or four weeks! But I can not stay here one half as long!' He fell back on the pillows, but went on urgently. 'I am here on the most important

120

matter! I have to find—I thank you, sir, for your help, but, I must continue on my way!'

'My dear sir, there can be no chance of your moving from here for some days. Already you have a little fever. To leave the bed would be madness. You would fall sick, and might be very ill indeed! And that on top of your broken arm—!'

Simon argued for some minutes more, but indeed he did feel very unwell, and in the end, he gave up protesting, determining to leave Signor Motta's care just as soon as he felt well enough. 'You are very kind, sir. And I accept your hospitality. I do not like to think what might have happened had you not come by!'

*   *   *

Simon's fever made him delirious that night, and he continued so for two days. Then the fever left him, and though weak, he began to mend quickly. Signor Motta was out for much of the day: Simon understood that he had a very extensive practice among the Genoese aristocracy, but he was not left alone. Signor Motta's sister, who was also his housekeeper, sat with him a good deal; and when she was otherwise occupied, the maid, whom Simon had seen the very first day, kept her eye upon him.

In the evenings, however, Signor Motta would come to sit and to talk with Simon. It seemed that Signor Motta had at one time spent nearly a year in England, which accounted for his excellent command of the English tongue, and now he was very happy to be able to practise the language and to learn what had happened in Britain since he had left it.

Simon was not only exceedingly grateful to the Italian, but also liked him, and the two soon became friends. And one evening, when he had been in the care of Signor Motta for some ten days, he confided to him the purpose of his visit to Italy.

'Ah! That explains much!' the Italian remarked. 'While you were delirious, you kept mentioning a name—it was Italian, but I could not quite catch it. I thought then, mio amico, that it was a particular lady for you!' And Signor Motta smiled archly.

'I do indeed seek a woman—but—not for the reason you thought. She is not an Italian, but English. Her name used to be Belleville, but I collect she married a—'

'Belleville! Did you say Belleville?' Signor Motta demanded excitedly.

'Yes. One Marguerite Belleville. Do you know her?'

'I—I have met her,' the Italian answered slowly.

'I hope she did not serve you as she has served others! As she is now attempting to serve my greatest friend!'

'No, no. Not I. I think I am not rich enough for la Belleville—I, a poor Genoese surgeon. But—I do know one whom she has injured—very terribly. But—before I can tell you the story, I must first ask permission of—of the family. It is not my story, you see.'

Simon urged the doctor to say more, but Signor Motta was adamant that he could say nothing until he had gained the consent of the person it concerned, and Simon had to be content.

The broken arm continued to mend very satisfactorily, and the bruising from the dislocated shoulder faded away, and Simon was at last allowed out of bed. For the first day or so, Simon had to remain indoors, and was not allowed to tire himself, and both Chiara Motta, the doctor's sister, and Maria-Elena, the maid, watched over him like the dragon guarding the apples of the Hesperides. Each evening, Simon demanded to know whether the doctor had permission to let him know of Marguerite Belleville's iniquities in Genoa, and each evening, Signor Motta shook his head.

Then Simon was allowed to walk out of doors for a little: only a few minutes on the first day, but gradually it was increased, and soon Simon felt quite his old self again, and was impatient to get on the trail of the infamous contessa.

But it was not till Simon had been for three

whole weeks a guest of the good doctor that Signor Motta announced, 'This evening, my friend, I shall take you visiting. And, I promise you, you will learn more than enough to— spike la Belleville's guns!' The Italian produced the English idiom with a humorous smile of triumph. 'You see, sir, she is wanted in this city for theft. Were she to return here—' And Signor Motta shook his head, and slowly drew his hand across his throat.

*   *   *

As the month of June drew towards its inevitable close, Kate and Lord Barnstaple did their very best to appear as usual when they were in society, but the strain could not be entirely hidden.

Lady Parton seemed to appear in Wimpole Street solely to comment on her niece's diminished looks. 'Really, Katherine, you hardly appear like a newly-betrothed girl. I can not remember when I have seen you less in looks. I have said it before, and I will say it again, anyone would think that Barnstaple is not quite attentive.' The gist of her ladyship's remarks was always the same.

'Thank you, ma'am, but I am very well,' Kate replied every time. 'It is just that I find the heat of the summer a little oppressive. It is very hot this year.'

On one occasion, Lady Parton turned to

Susan who was also in the room. 'Do not you think your sister sadly pulled down, niece? You are in looks indeed, as I would expect you to be; but Katherine has lost what little looks she had, do not you agree?'

Susan was not a particularly perceptive sister, but she could be relied upon to dislike her aunt's attempts to interfere. 'I had not noticed, ma'am. Kate seems quite the same as always to me.'

'Ah,' Lady Parton smiled knowingly, 'that is because you are so happy yourself that you have not time to see others about you. It is always so when a happy marriage is in the offing.'

'I assure you, ma'am,' Kate said somewhat austerely, 'I am perfectly well.'

She would have liked to assure her aunt that a happy marriage was in the offing for her also, but the month was drawing too rapidly to its close, and still there was no news from Mr. Borrowdale. Kate could well see that she might indeed be called upon to break her engagement with Lord Barnstaple, and she liked the idea less and less.

Still, she did not have to do so yet! She added, very firmly, 'Yes, perfectly well. Lord Barnstaple and I agree together perfectly.'

'I hope that may be so,' her aunt returned disparagingly. 'If you say it is so, I suppose I must believe you. But really, niece, no-one would guess it from your appearance!'

*　　*　　*

That rumours were circulating in society that all was not well between Lord Barnstaple and his betrothed was an acknowledged fact between the two concerned. Kate suspected her aunt of starting them, for that lady was still chagrined that her own daughter had been passed over without a second glance. Lord Barnstaple himself favoured the countess.

They saw that lady almost every day. Whenever they drove in the Park they would be sure to see her, escorted by the Baron Marsfold or by Lord Rupert Pelly, or by another of their rackety set. But once or twice she was seen to be escorted by a more respectable member of society. When she was seen in the company of an heir to a dukedom, Kate said hopefully, 'Perhaps, my lord, the countess will let you escape after all. I am sure she would prefer strawberry leaves to any other coronet!'

'That puppy is young enough to be her son!'

'Oh, surely not, my lord!'

'The countess was nearly thirty when I knew her before,' Richard said ungallantly. 'You may be sure his parents will put a stop to it, for the sake of the title, if for no other reason.' He looked at Kate gloomily; 'I am afraid we may expect no such relief.'

And Kate could not help being affected by

the earl's pessimism, though she did her utmost not to show it.

Lord Netley himself was by no means a careless father, and his Kate's despondency had not escaped his notice. He had no wish for his daughter to be made unhappy for life, and at last he made up his mind to find out if she wished to go through with her engagement to the Earl of Barnstaple.

Accordingly, he summoned her to the library one morning after breakfast.

'Now, look here, Kate my dear,' he began, 'it seems to me that there is something amiss with you. You have made attempts to appear cheerful, I have seen that, but when you think yourself unregarded your countenance looks quite otherwise. So, I want you to tell me straightly, do you want to call off this arrangement with Barnstaple? I remember that you told me that—that it was a business arrangement, and if you like someone else better—?'

'Oh, no, sir! No! I do not want to call it off in the least!'

'If you are worried about the tattling there would be, do not regard it. It is better far to break off an engagement, than find yourself leg-shackled for life to a man you can not abide!'

'But—I like Lord Barnstaple very well, Papa!'

'Then, can not you tell me what it is that ails

you? I can not deny that rumours have reached me that all is not well between you. If it is Barnstaple himself who is trying to slide out of his commitment, I will soon bring him to heel! He will not treat one of *my* daughters as if she were some—some Cyprian he has tired of!' And Lord Netley looked extremely vexed, and his face swelled up red like a turkey-cock's.

'Oh, no, sir! Lord Barnstaple would never do anything so dishonourable!'

'But—I can see that something is not right!' Lord Netley looked wistful. 'I wish you would confide in me, Kate.'

Her father's look touched Kate's heart, and she would have given much to tell her father everything. But of course, that was not possible. She said brokenly, 'Really, there is nothing sir!'

Lord Netley reached out and caught hold of his daughter's hand. 'You know, my dear, since your mother departed from us, I have tried my best to take her place. With a son, I might have managed better, but with six daughters— But—I have seen you all grow into beautiful women, with good hearts and pleasant manners, so—what more could I ask? But, it is at times like this, that I feel you need a mother's care.'

'Oh, Papa!' Kate was weeping now. Her father rarely mentioned his wife, and it was a sign that he was moved that he did so now.

'You have been the best father we could have had!'

Her father smiled and patted her hand. 'Well, I can say that throughout I have always had the happiness of you girls as my first consideration. So—if there is anything I can do for you, my dear . . . ?'

Kate gave no answer, but hugged her father.

Lord Netley sighed. 'Well, if you do wish to confide in me later, my dear, I shall always be here. And, if you do wish to break it off with Barnstaple, then you have only to tell me. I will do all that is necessary, and you need have no part of it. You can go back to Netcombe early, and escape the tittle-tattle, and I will make all right with Barnstaple.'

'I promise you, Papa, I do not wish to break if off in the least!' Kate sobbed.

'If you are sure, my dear.'

Kate fled to her room, and there relieved her tense feelings by indulging in a good cry. It was something of which she was rarely guilty, but now her heart was too full. If Lord Barnstaple did not hear from Mr. Borrowdale very shortly, then she would indeed have to break her engagement with his lordship and—

It came to Kate, with lightning swiftness, that what she wanted of all things was to be Lord Barnstaple's wife: not merely because she did not wish him to fall a prey to the countess, but because she was in love with him.

As the thought came to her, she sat up

straight with surprise. She had been a ninnyhammer not to realize it before. Quite when she had fallen out of love with Sir James Brocket and into love with the Earl of Barnstaple she did not know. But now she knew well enough that she would do anything for the earl's good, and it seemed that the greatest sacrifice she could make was to be demanded of her.

From realizing the truth about her own feelings, Kate wondered gloomily just what the earl might feel for her. Respect, she thought, but—certainly not love. The betrothal had been a matter of business, and she could not think that he had changed.

*   *   *

When the earl came to Wimpole Street later that day, Kate was conscious that for the first time there was a fluttering in her stomach as she greeted him, and the hand that she held out was trembling.

Richard carried her hand to his lips. 'Kate!'

'My lord! You have news?'

Richard shook his head, and Kate felt a surge of love and pity as she looked into his face. Anxiety and worry were plainly to be seen, but not, she thought sadly, any tender feelings for herself. But there was something else there also, a new fire in the earl's eyes: a new resolution.

'I have made up my mind, Kate!' Richard announced. 'I am catching the next packet for France. I mean to follow Simon's route. I am convinced that something is amiss. He knew how important his mission was; he would never leave us without news for so long. He may be ill. He may have been attacked by brigands. I do not know. But I can rest no longer. I must go myself and find out!'

Kate's own heart beat quickly in her breast. 'Oh, my lord!' She knew not what else to say.

'Had it not been for the scandal that would have raged about your own head, Kate, I would have bid the countess do her worst! I care not for myself now. Were all the opprobrium to fall upon myself, I would not care; I would marry you, Kate, without the least care in the world! But, you would inevitably be dragged down with me, Kate; and I could not bear that!'

'But—I—I would be willing to face it, my lord!' Kate cried, wondering if she could indeed ever let his lordship go now.

'I would never agree to that, my dear! You have been the staunchest, truest friend that a man ever had! No-one could have tried harder than you to help me escape the results of youthful folly. But, it is *my* folly, Kate, and it is not right that you should pay the price also. You have done more than any man would have had the right to expect from the woman most truly attached to him by all the tenderest ties.

131

But, from a woman who has no such ties, and now, I make no doubt, but little respect either, I can not, and I will not ask for more! Or, indeed, accept it!' And the earl looked immoveable.

His words were as a knife twisting in Kate's heart. He believed that she did not care for him. Oh! If only he knew how different the truth was! But then—he cared nothing for her, and knowledge of her love could only be an embarrassment to him.

'I—I would do anything I could, my lord—' Kate attempted to speak resolutely.

But Richard shook his head. 'No, my dear. I have no right to ask for any sacrifice more. You have—'

'But—I have made no sacrifice! I have been happy—'

'Oh, my dear—dearest Kate, our arrangement was a purely practical one, have you forgot? Most women, in such a situation, would have withdrawn at the beginning, and left me to my fate. But you have stood by me—'

'And have you forgot, my lord, that it was I who first proposed the arrangement?' Kate returned forcing herself to speak lightly.

'No, I have not forgot. Nor how I answered you at the first. I see now that I should have stuck to it; then you would have escaped this imbroglio.'

'You would say, my lord, that I have been

but a burden to you?' Kate attempted to speak lightly, but her voice faltered.

'Never, my dear! You have given me strength and friendship; I shall be in your debt forever. Now, listen to me, dear Kate. I shall do my best to find Simon, and to return to England before the end of the month. But, if I am not returned, then you must announce that your betrothal to me is broken off. What the countess does then, I care not. You must tell her that you know not where I am nor when I shall return. She will not be able to start an action against me if I am not here.'

'But—where do you mean to go, my lord?'

'Perhaps across the Atlantic once more. I fled there from her once!'

'Oh, no, my lord! You must not give way to her!'

'I promise that if I can return in time with good news, nothing but death shall keep me away! But I am determined that I shall never marry the Countess Snaguingrazzo!'

A little warmth touched Kate's frozen heart at this.

But the earl did not remain much longer. He bade her farewell, and hurried off to take horse to Dover.

'I hate to leave you to face everything alone!'

'I shall be very well, my lord! Only do you return in time—and with some news—and with Mr. Borrowdale. May God preserve him!'

'Amen to that!' Richard answered, and caught Kate's hand once more before he hurried off.

CHAPTER EIGHT

Kate's wretchedness at the earl's departure may be imagined: not only did she fear for his safety, traversing, as he was, wild areas known to be full of roving bands of banditti, but, conscious now of her changed feelings towards him, she would wish to be with him at all times, and his absence could cause nothing but sorrow.

The earl did not, however, leave her totally abandoned, for he sent her frequent—daily reports; messages scribbled wherever he paused for the night. Eagerly she snatched them up as they were delivered to her; eagerly she perused them, but always her hopes were dashed.

Lord Barnstaple reported getting onto Simon Borrowdale's track easily enough: that young man had travelled by the fastest route through France, and the earl followed as swiftly as hired horses would allow. When he reached Italy, the earl found that his friend had started to make numerous enquiries, for there were many ostlers and waiters and chamber-maids who remembered the yellow-headed Englishman who had asked a great many questions about a beautiful lady. Most of them smiled as they spoke of him to the earl, thinking the interest of both to be quite other than it was.

But at Genoa the trail grew cold. The earl wasted two days there, following up the many rumours which reached him, but none of which led to Mr. Borrowdale; and in the end, feeling very uneasy, the earl continued his way to Florence, praying to come upon the trail again there.

Kate read and re-read the earl's missives: when she had learnt his news, she studied the letters again, searching, hoping, for some sign of more than mere friendly, respectful feeling on the earl's part towards herself. But Kate always searched in vain; she was destined to be disappointed in that also. Nevertheless, the letters were very precious to her, and she locked them all away in her desk, and sometimes took them out, not in order to read them again, but merely to hold them, and feel that the earl was near.

Of course Kate had to endure a great many questions about Lord Barnstaple when his absence from London became known. Her friends regarded her with loving pity: those who were not so well disposed, with a greater or lesser degree of malicious triumph. We told you how it would be, they seemed to say. How could you expect that *you* would be able to hold such a man as the earl?

To all Kate told the same story: that the earl had had to leave London in order to attend to certain business affairs; but it was obvious that few believed her. She saw her father's kindly, questioning looks; but the viscount made no attempt to ask direct questions now.

Lady Parton, on the other hand, was forever mentioning the subject.

'And have you heard from the earl today, Katherine?' she would demand, plainly expecting a negative answer. 'And where is his lordship now? Surely he must return to you soon! He has been away an age. I must say, if *I* were in your shoes, I should not take kindly to being deserted so.'

And Kate would answer with as bright a mien as she could that she had indeed received a letter from his lordship, who was well, but still engaged upon his affairs, and would not be returning to London yet.

But when she was able to escape to her own room, Kate shed many bitter tears.

As was only to be expected the Countess Snaguingrazzo had waylaid her as soon as the earl's absence was known, and demanded to know where he was. The occasion was at the Opera, and she caught hold of Kate as the girl was making her way back to the family box after the first interval, with the result that Kate missed a good deal of the second act.

The countess drew Kate into one of the

now-empty refreshment-rooms, and voiced her suspicions in no uncertain manner.

'I demand that you tell me at once where Richard is!' she cried.

'I am unable to do that, ma'am, for I do not know.'

'Oh, fudge! Of course you know! Tell me at once!'

'Indeed, ma'am, I do not know where the earl is at the moment!'

'Oh, I know well enough that it is some scheme by which Richard thinks to escape me. But, I tell you, Miss Katherine, I shall have the earl in the end, for, if I do not, I can promise you that there will be such a scandal burst about his head, the like of which has never been heard in London before!' And here the countess had taken hold of Kate's arm and shaken it to emphasise her words.

Kate pulled her arm away and said with dignity, 'I make no doubt but that you will do it, ma'am, if you are able—'

'Oh, I am able, all right!' the countess broke in. 'You forget that I have nothing to lose, but that Richard has everything! But he has spurned me and must pay the price. How dare he think that he can treat me, Marguerite Belleville, as if I were some common Cyprian! He begged me to marry him once, and he shall do so again, I promise you! When he learns what will happen to him if he does not—' And the countess raved on for some time in this fashion, her determination to pay out the earl for having rejected her thudding in Kate's ears.

The girl felt sick as she listened, and feared that she might lose consciousness, so faint did she feel, but she clung to her composure and heard the countess out.

When the other woman paused for breath, Kate, without any expectation of success, but feeling for the earl's sake that she must make some attempt, said very reasonably, 'I had thought your real desire was to enter society, ma'am?'

'And so it was,' the countess returned, panting after her recent exertions, '—so it was—at the beginning—'

'Such could still be arranged,' Kate went on pleasantly; 'I feel certain that it could. After all, I have seen you in company with Lord Banstead, and the Marquis of Darrington, and—and the heir to the Duke of Peebleshire . . .'

The countess preened herself a little. 'That is true. I have never had the least difficulty in attracting the attentions of gentlemen. What of it?'

'Are not you then already *in* society, ma'am? I can not see that Lord Barnstaple would be able to introduce you any higher.'

'Pah! You know well enough that to be seen driving in the Park with a young blade, however nobly born, is not the same thing as being invited to dine at their table. I wish to be a respectable member of society now, Miss

Katherine, accepted—acknowledged by the women as well as the men. For it is the women, as you well know, Miss Katherine, who rule society.'

'Then I could help you to such recognition, ma'am,' Kate said eagerly. 'My aunt, Lady Parton, would receive you, I am certain—' Kate had no belief that she herself could persuade her aunt to such a course, but she might well persuade her father to persuade his sister. '—she is to give a ball in two weeks' time. I will procure a card for you willingly—'

'I told you before that that is no longer enough! I wish for an established position, with an unassailable title of my own, a house suitable for entertaining—I have a mind to hold a salon, Miss Katherine.'

'But—if you ruin Lord Barnstaple, you will never achieve your aim!'

'But I shall have had the satisfaction of humbling Richard's pride!'

'But why? If in doing so, you injure yourself!'

'Oh, you should have known him, Miss Katherine, as he once was! You would understand me then! He adored me! He idolized me! He worshipped me! He was my puppydog: my slave. But now—' The countess's eyes flashed angrily, I mean to see him humble again.'

Kate was not only disgusted, her heart bled—not only for the earl, but for herself. She wished that the earl might feel for her what he had once felt for this heartless, shameless creature. But she swallowed her loathing, and remained sometime longer, attempting to use the countess's self-interest to triumph over her malevolence.

But all was in vain. However she put the argument, whatever inducements she proffered, even to the extent of promising that her godfather, the Duke of Wellington himself, should dance the waltz with the countess at Almack's, the countess was not to be moved from her fixed determination, either to become the Countess of Barnstaple, or to drag the earl into the mire for her vengeance on him for her supposed wrongs.

Sick at heart, Kate at last returned to her party, but saw and heard almost nothing of the remainder of the opera, for her eyes were blinded by tears, and her thoughts were thousands of miles away with Lord Barnstaple.

*   *   *

If at the first Kate could have made no complaint that the earl failed to keep her informed of his progress, suddenly, just before the last days of June, his regular communications ceased.

Up to now, Kate had been accustomed to receiving a letter from him every day, and though they had brought no good news, she

140

had rejoiced in them as being evidence that his lordship had her always in his thoughts.

But when such letters ceased, Kate grew frantic. The first day on which no letter arrived was uncomfortable enough, but she was able to console herself with the thought that it was scarcely to be wondered at that letters from as far away as Florence should be delayed.

When there was nothing the next day either, Kate began to worry in a hopeless way she had not worried before; and by the end of the third day without news, she was almost prostrate with anxiety. Both Mr. Borrowdale and now the earl seemed to have disappeared without trace, and Kate was left to brood on whatever terrible fate her fecund imagination presented to her.

Had it been possible for her to confide in someone, things would have been much eased for her. But of course, it was not possible. She could not disclose to anyone how things really were. It was not her secret, and in any case, the whole purpose of all they were doing was to keep the real state of affairs concealed. Kate had to bear everything quite alone now.

Her cousin Marjory, who had admired Lord Barnstaple so much, and who at first had been good-naturedly envious of her cousin's greater luck, now looked at her sympathetically, and blurted out, 'Mamma says Lord Barnstaple is regretting asking for you, but I told her that I do not believe it, Kate! After all, men do have

141

affairs to keep them from home, and his lordship has not been gone so very long!'

'You are a kind soul, Marjory, and I promise you the earl does not regret what he has done. He will be home again very soon, I promise you!'

But Kate could not help thinking wryly that things had come to a pretty pass when she was the object of pity of her cousin.

Once or twice, she did almost tell her father, but she drew back from the disclosure, hoping against hope that all would turn out well.

*   *   *

So the last days of the month passed in a cloud of misery for Kate. And the misery was not made any better by her constantly seeing the Contessa Snaguingrazzo: in the Park, and at the theatre, or shopping in a fashionable street. Although the countess did not seek to speak to her again, Kate could not but be aware of the countess's complacent, triumphant smile, which seemed to grow even broader as the month drew towards its close.

Now Kate had to acknowledge to herself that she had all but given up hope. Of course she still longed for the earl to arrive—or even communicate with her, but—she hardly dared hope now.

Kate awoke on the final day of June exhausted in body and spirit, and oppressed by the knowledge that the day was come at last when she would have to ask her father to publish the announcement that her betrothal to Lord Barnstaple was broken off.

She was conscious of a sad headache when she woke, and it grew worse as the morning proceeded. At breakfast Kate said hardly a word, except to ask her father if she might have an interview with him afterwards.

The viscount replied that he was engaged for some time, but that he expected to be free some time after noon.

Kate knew not whether to be pleased or happy at the delay. She was given thereby a few more hours in which to hope against hope that there might be news from the earl, but hope, Kate had come to think, was a treacherous friend, ever disappointing her.

Somehow the morning passed. To prevent herself being alone when her thoughts were torture to her, Kate went out, ostensibly to shop, but in reality to walk swiftly, first to Bond Street, then back again taking a very circuitous route, even hurrying through Manchester Square before she turned in again at her father's door in Wimpole Street.

Resolutely she went to her father's study as soon as she had removed her bonnet, and entered the room with a dead heart. Her father, she saw at once, looked pleased. Engravings were scattered on his desk, and the viscount was consulting a heavy folio volume.

'Oh! I am sorry to disturb you, Papa.'

'Not at all, my dear,' Lord Netley said with a kind look, plainly lying. 'Come in. I remember you asked to speak to me.'

Kate nodded and took a deep breath.

'Come and sit down.' And Lord Netley swept a chair free of yet more prints.

'These are new prints, Papa?'

'Yes, my dear. They have just arrived from Michaelson's. I am checking them against this catalogue.'

The viscount looked at his daughter expectantly. He waited patiently, unwilling to force his daughter, whom he saw well enough, was far from happy.

'Well, Kate?' he said at last.

But Kate stared at the prints, unable to begin.

'You are missing Barnstaple, my dear?' the viscount ventured at last.

Kate nodded again, and hid her face, looking down at the hands clasped in her lap.

'You have heard from him?'

This time Kate shook her head.

'You have—quarrelled, my dear?'

'Oh, no, Papa! Nothing like that!' Her look now was so direct that the viscount was certain his daughter was telling the truth,

'Well, then; I dare say he will come home as soon as he may, Kate.'

'It—it is not quite so easy as that, Papa,' Kate said slowly.

'No? Then, pray tell me, my dear, what it is that troubles you, for—a trouble shared is a trouble halved, you know!'

But the girl remained silent, plainly much upset, and the viscount watched the emotions fleeting across her face. Then he said gently, 'Am I so hard to speak with, my dear?'

'Oh, no, Papa! It is not that! It is—' And then Kate's feelings became too much for her, and tears began to trickle down her cheeks.

'Oh, my dear child!'

'I am sorry, Papa! I am just being foolish!' And Kate tried to wipe away the tears.

Much moved, Lord Netley put his arms round his daughter, comforting her silently.

It was while they were standing so that a footman came to say that the Countess Snaguingrazzo had called to see Miss Katherine Netley.

At once Kate, stricken, looked up, clinging to her father's hand.

'Pray tell the countess that Miss Katherine is not at home,' the viscount said testily.

But Kate shook her head. 'No, Papa. I must see the countess. It is the last day of June today, and I can no longer put it off.' She turned to the servant. 'Pray tell her ladyship that I will be with her directly. You may show her into the library.'

The servant bowed and disappeared, and Lord Netley remarked, 'There really is no need, my dear.'

The viscount would have said more, but Kate broke in, 'I must see her, Papa. But first I will tell you why she is come.' And then, after obtaining her father's promise of the strictest secrecy, Kate told her father, very briefly, the whole story, and what the countess meant to do if she did not have her way.

The viscount was immediately incensed, not only with the countess but also with the earl, and Kate was quick to spring to his defence.

'It is *I* who mean to give up Lord Barnstaple, Papa!' she cried. 'You must see that I can do nothing else! I have told him that I do not care if my name is dragged through the courts, but he could not bear it for my sake—and I could not bear it for his! So—what else can I do? I had hoped that Mr. Borrowdale would come back with some information which would make it impossible for the countess to marry Lord Barnstaple, but—now the end of the month is come, and we have heard nothing from him for weeks, and now the earl is vanished also— and—Oh, Papa! I must break it off. If I do not, the countess will make us all the gossip of London—'

'I have never heard anything so disgraceful!' Lord Netley cried. 'Do you mean to say that Barnstaple has been writing to this woman all the time he was engaged to you!'

'No, Papa! He has not! But the countess claims that he has!'

The viscount protested a good deal very
146

hotly, threatening to make public the countess's infamy, but Kate begged him to do nothing, reminding him of his promise of silence. 'I could not bear to be the one to bring scandal upon Lord Barnstaple's name, Papa!'

'Humph! Well, I can not like it, Kate. But I shall come with you when you interview this creature.'

'Oh, no, Papa! I would not have you drawn into this scrape.'

'It seems to me to be a great deal more than a scrape, my dear, and I would not dream of letting you go through with it alone. We will face this countess together, my dear.'

*   *   *

When they arrived in the library, they found that the lady was not alone. Standing beside her, bending over to speak to her and smiling ingratiatingly was a swarthy creature, whose garments betokened something of the dandy. He straightened as Kate and her father entered, and transferred his smile to them.

'Good morning, ma'am,' Kate greeted the countess, in quiet command of herself again; 'I regret having kept you waiting. Pray allow me to present my father, Lord Netley.'

The countess, dressed in a deep shade of pink which set off her dark hair and eyes, smiled brilliantly at the viscount and offered him her hand. Lord Netley would much have preferred not to take it, but habit was too strong for him. He took the countess's hand, but only bent over it formally.

The countess's eyes flashed, and her smile grew more intimate. 'My lord,' she murmured throatily, 'I am delighted to meet you.' She fluttered her eyelashes, and in spite of himself, the viscount had to admit that the countess was a damned fine woman.

Kate glanced at the man accompanying the countess, and felt at once that she would not have trusted him with so much as a farthing. He looked too ingratiating, and she disliked his oily hair as much as his oily smile, and she could hardly bring herself to give him even the slightest bow of acknowledgement, when the countess presented him as her lawyer, Mr. Begby.

The man bowed, and redoubled his detestably unctuous smile and proclaimed himself honoured to meet his lordship and his elegant daughter.

Kate then seated herself, but the viscount went to stand by the fireplace, resting one elbow upon the mantleshelf. His rather stocky figure emanated a suppressed belligerence, and a determination to see if he could that right was done by his own.

Mr. Begby, meanwhile, was still bowing and smiling and declaring his sensibility of the honour now being done him; but the countess broke in impatiently, 'I collect, Miss

Katherine, that you have acquainted his lordship with the purpose of my visit?'

'My father is aware of what you intend, ma'am,' Kate said icily.

Mr. Begby looked apologetically at Lord Netley. 'My client feels that in the circumstances—'

But again the countess broke across her lawyer's words. She looked at the viscount with heaving bosom, and her magnificent eyes flashed. 'My lord,' she said in trembling tones which demanded pity, 'you see before you a much wronged woman.' And the countess touched her eyes with another of her delicate, lace-edged handkerchieves. 'I have suffered much, my lord.' And she glanced at the viscount from under lowered lashes to see if her appeal to him had had the desired effect.

But Lord Netley was not one whit impressed. At least, his eyes told him that he was in the presence of a very beautiful woman, but his heart was not touched in the slightest. All the mothering instincts he had been forced to develop since the death of his wife were roused: he was like a lioness in defence of her young. 'It seems, ma'am, that you would now wish to make my daughter suffer also,' he returned curtly.

The countess raised her hands in deprecation. 'No, no, my lord! I have no wish—not the least in the world—to harm Miss Katherine. That is not my desire at all.'

149

'Well, you are going a strange way about things then, ma'am!' And Lord Netley glared at the countess.

'Her ladyship is interested only in claiming what is justly hers,' Mr. Begby now put in with a placating smile.

'I dispute that,' the viscount retorted sharply. 'Lord Barnstaple is engaged to my daughter, and so all the world knows.'

'But that does not alter my client's position, my lord. The Earl of Barnstaple paid his addresses to the Countess Snaguingrazzo before his betrothal to Miss Katherine was announced. My client was convinced of the earl's integrity. She has indeed the prior claim.'

'We have *both* been exceedingly ill-used by his lordship,' the countess now proclaimed, attempting a brave look. 'My heart bleeds for your daughter, sir. She has been deceived by a most accomplished creature—'

'In that case, I wonder you would wish to attach yourself to him!'

'Ah, my lord! Defenceless woman as I am, I must claim protection where I may. And, as Mr. Begby says, I have the prior claim.'

'And what proof have you of that, ma'am? All the world knows that Barnstaple never had the least intention of marrying until—until he asked for my daughter's hand!'

'Certainly that is what he led the world to believe, my lord, but in that the world was

150

deceived. I have countless proofs to the contrary. I have known his lordship from long ago, and it was because I was not able to marry him years ago that he has remained a bachelor all this time. I was married then, my lord, to my first husband, Joseph Belleville. The earl, he was plain Richard Dunthrop then, begged me to go away with him. But, I could not be so careless of the customs of society and the church, my lord. I was married in holy wedlock to Joseph Belleville, and I could not go in the face of all I held most sacred—whatever may have been my personal wishes—the wishes of my heart.' And the countess lowered her eyes, and placed one hand delicately on that part of her anatomy.

Kate had been listening in silence, having not uttered one word since she had presented her father. But now disgust overcame her, and she burst out, 'That is not what I have heard, ma'am! Were his lordship here, he would tell a very different story!'

The countess turned to the young girl, every lineament of her face expressive of pity and understanding. 'Of course he would, my dear. And of course I do understand, my dear Miss Katherine, how very unpleasing it must be to you to hear that the man you love has for years been hopelessly, desperately in love with another—'

'I assure you, ma'am, you quite mistake the matter,' Kate broke in. 'The Earl of

Barnstaple did love you once, it is true, when he was young. But since that time, he has learnt what you really are, ma'am! You deceived him then, just as you are attempting to deceive him now! He wanted none of you then, and will have none of you now!'

An expression of fury crossed the countess's face, but it was gone as soon as it had come. 'I understand your anger, dear Miss Katherine,' she said soothingly. 'But, you know only half the story. I can produce sufficient proofs of Lord Barnstaple's feelings for me to satisfy the most exacting creature.'

Mr. Begby now delved into a case he had with him, and produced two or three pieces of paper. 'Here, Miss Katherine, my lord, is the proof to which my client refers. Letters from his lordship to my client, which amply confirm my client's claim.'

Making not the slightest effort to take the papers from Mr. Begby, Kate said contemptuously, 'I have no wish to see them, sir. I do not believe in their authenticity.'

Mr. Begby now offered the papers to Lord Netley who took them, glanced at the contents briefly, then went over to one of the windows and held each paper up to the light in turn.

Kate did not watch her father, but kept her eyes on the ground, a frown upon her brow. But the countess and Mr. Begby both watched the viscount, the former with alertness, the

152

latter with his unctuous smile.

After some moments, Lord Netley turned back to them. 'One of the papers I will accept as genuine. The other two are clearly forgeries,' he remarked dismissively, holding out the papers to Begby.

'What do you mean, my lord!' the countess cried. 'Are you trying to say that those papers were not written to me by the present Earl of Barnstaple!'

'Who wrote them, ma'am, I can not say; but I repeat, one of those letters may well be genuine. Two, however, are clearly forgeries.' And the viscount emphasised the last word. He glanced briefly at his daughter, who was staring at him in amazement, and gave her a reassuring smile.

Mr. Begby now said with a deprecating smile, 'I beg your pardon, my lord, but there must be some mistake. My client received those letters from the present Earl of Barnstaple seventeen years ago, when he was plain Richard Dunthrop.'

'And *I* beg *your* pardon, sir, but I assure you, only one of those letters can have been written at the time you mention. The other two are quite plainly more recent productions—copies of real letters, perhaps, but certainly not penned in the year in which they purport to have been written. And, if you have any thought of using them in any legal way, I should advise you to drop the plan at once.

153

You would be laughed out of court.'

'But how can you be so certain, my lord?' Mr. Begby began.

But the countess broke in before the viscount had time to answer, 'But—you accept one of the letters as genuine, my lord?'

Lord Netley regarded the countess for a moment in silence. 'Of the time, ma'am,' he said meaningly.

'And in that, I think you will agree that the writer made his feelings quite plain?'

'Certainly. But I would add, seventeen years is a long time, ma'am. People change in that time.'

'I have more recent declarations,' the countess returned impatiently. 'Produce them, Begby.'

The lawyer was already delving into his case. Now he drew out other papers and offered them to Lord Netley, who took them and glanced at them negligently.

'They are forgeries also, Papa!' Kate exclaimed agitatedly. 'Lord *Barnstaple* has never written to the countess. All communication ceased seventeen years ago!'

'So he has told you, my dear,' the countess smiled sweetly. 'But those letters prove otherwise.'

'That is not true!' Kate flared. 'His lordship loathes you!'

'My dear Miss Katherine,' the countess went on in the same kindly tone, 'he was bound to say that to you, was not he? But only read those letters!'

'They are forgeries, I say!'

'Ah! And can you prove it?'

Kate looked at her father anxiously. 'Papa?'

Swiftly Lord Netley scanned the papers again, then held them up to the light and scrutinised them more carefully. 'I can not tell, my dear. They may or may not be genuine. It would be Barnstaple's word against the Countess Snaguingrazzo's.'

'But—you would not wish it to come to that, would you, my lord?' the countess said persuasively. 'Much better, I am sure you agree, to keep it out of court, and your daughter's name free from scandal.'

'You also would be touched by the scandal, ma'am.'

The countess shrugged. 'I have been wronged, my lord. I want justice.'

Lord Netley turned to his daughter. 'Well, Kate?'

Kate had been listening to the passage between her father and the countess, close to tears. Now she made an effort to compose herself, but there was a break in her voice as she declared, 'For myself I do not care, Papa. But I can not expose his lordship to all the indignity and ignominy that would ensue were the—the countess to bring an action for breach of promise.'

'I knew you would be sensible, my dear,' the

155

countess exclaimed in a satisfied voice. 'You have avoided a great deal of unpleasantness for us all.' She turned to the viscount. 'Tell me, my lord, what is it that makes you believe that only one of my early letters from Lord Barnstaple is genuine?'

The viscount shrugged. 'The paper, ma'am. That type of paper did not exist before eighteen-fifteen. Therefore, anything purporting to be before that date must be a forgery.'

The countess gave the viscount an odd look. 'Careless,' she murmured. Then she continued in business-like tones. 'Now, my lord, you will put the notice in the Morning Post directly?'

Lord Netley glared at the countess. '*I* have not agreed to anything yet, ma'am. But I promise you this, I shall make certain every door in London is closed against you. You would be another Lady Blessington.'

'I seem to recall that some of the highest names of the land are to be found in her salon, my lord.'

'But the lady herself is received nowhere, ma'am.'

Kate heard her father in astonishment. Never before had she heard such ruthlessness in his voice.

But the countess seemed unaffected by it. 'I would advise you, my lord, to act quickly. I have waited long enough already. I do not choose to wait longer.'

'Do not you threaten *me*, ma'am!' Lord Netley cried, his face growing red with choler. 'I have not yet decided if I shall permit my daughter to withdraw—'

'Papa!'

But what might have ensued was to remain unknown, for at that moment a footman entered, and announced to Kate, 'Mr. Borrowdale is come, ma'am, and is asking to see you.'

CHAPTER NINE

'What the devil do you mean by interrupting us?' Lord Netley demanded, incensed.

But Kate ran towards the servant. 'Mr. Borrowdale! *Mr. Borrowdale,* you say! Oh, pray bring him here at once!'

'We don't want young Borrowdale here now, Kate!' the viscount went on impatiently.

'Oh, but Papa! We do! We do! He must bring news!' Kate turned back to the footman who had been hesitating, looking from the girl to his master. 'Hurry, John! Hurry!'

The man went out swiftly at Kate's urging, and the girl then turned to her father. 'I told you, Papa, how Mr. Borrowdale went to Italy on behalf of Lord Barnstaple. And that Lord Barnstaple went after him, so worried was he when he heard nothing after Genoa—'

The viscount looked at his daughter's anxious, hopeful face and his own countenance broke into a smile. 'I had forgot, my dear. I pray he may bring good news.'

The door opened then—the footman had indeed hurried—and Mr. Borrowdale was announced. As soon as that young man's yellow head appeared, Kate ran to him, holding out her hands. 'Oh, sir! You are safe! We had near given up hope!'

Mr. Borrowdale clasped Kate's hands with his one free hand, his smiling face now anxious. 'Given up hope, Miss Katherine! But—did not you receive my message?'

Kate shook her head, then seemed to become aware of the sling supporting Mr. Borrowdale's right arm. 'You are injured, sir!'

'An unfortunate break, only; and it is mending well, ma'am, I thank you. But because of it, I had to get another to write my letters for me. And Dick has not received my messages, you say?'

'Lord Barnstaple is not here, sir. He went to Italy after you, so worried was he when he heard nothing from you. Have not you seen him then, sir?'

'Dick in Italy! But I have not seen him since that night I left London!'

Kate's heart sank as quickly now as it had risen when she heard Mr. Borrowdale had come.

Mr. Borrowdale understood her distressed

look, and gripped her hands consolingly. 'Do not you worry about Dick, ma'am. He can look after himself. He will come back right as a trivet, you will see. But—I have news, ma'am!' And Mr. Borrowdale looked down at her excitedly. Then, over the girl's shoulder he became aware of the countess and Mr. Begby. He turned back to Kate anxiously. 'Oh, Miss Katherine! I am not too late—I hope!'

'No, no! That is—nothing has been settled yet.'

The countess now began to protest, but no-one took any notice of her. Lord Netley stepped forward, holding out his hand to Simon Borrowdale, his face grave and unsmiling. 'Borrowdale. I hope I see you well. You have some concern in this business, I collect?'

Mr. Borrowdale bowed. 'My lord, I beg you to excuse me—' His eyes strayed to the countess once more, then back to his lordship's face. I have indeed news.'

Kate smiled at that, and tried to feel confident that Lord Barnstaple was safe and well. 'Oh, sir!'

The countess now spoke firmly, and in a voice that forced attention. 'My lord, I am not prepared to wait here longer. I am not accustomed to being ignored. If you wish to hear the story of this young man's adventures, I do not.' The woman rose, and spoke in a voice which made it plain that she considered there was no more to be said. 'You know the situation, my lord. If a notice does not appear in the next edition of the Morning Post, announcing the breaking off of the betrothal between your daughter and Lord Barnstaple, you know well what consequences will follow. I hope you will be—prudent, my lord.' The countess gave the viscount a meaning look, then arranged her veil deliberately, before turning to her lawyer. 'Come, Begby. There is nothing more to be said.'

The lawyer smiled ingratiatingly, then bowed to the viscount and to Kate, before following his client. But the countess had taken only a pace or two forward when she was stopped by Mr. Borrowdale placing his person in her path.

'Let me pass, sir!' the countess cried imperiously.

'Allow me to present myself, ma am. Simon Borrowdale, Dick Dunsford's oldest—and I dare say—best friend.' And he bowed.

The countess barely acknowledged his words with the merest inclination of her head, and made to step forward again.

'One moment, ma'am,' Simon Borrowdale said firmly. 'A moment ago you said that you had no wish to hear the story of my adventures, But, I must beg you to wait, ma'am. I think you will find them of more than usual interest. Indeed, I flatter myself you will find them quite spellbinding.' And Mr.

Borrowdale smiled in an easy way.

'How so, sir?'

'As you have heard, ma'am, I have been in Italy. And while there, I had the pleasure of meeting someone—intimately acquainted with you, ma'am.'

'I have no wish to meet any persons from that country. I have no intimate acquaintances there. You have been imposed upon, sir.'

'I think not, ma'am. They were able to relate to me in such detail the history of their dealings with you. You will like to hear of them again, I am convinced.'

'Let me pass, sir!' And for the third time the countess attempted to get past Simon.

'When you have heard everything, ma'am,' Simon smiled engagingly.

'Begby, I wish to leave!' the countess said imperiously to the lawyer.

'Of course, my lady.' He turned to Simon. 'I must beg you, sir, to let the lady pass.'

'Certainly. In due time.'

'Remove him, Begby!'

The lawyer looked decidedly taken aback at the order, for even one-handed Simon Borrowdale was a formidable opponent. 'Perhaps it would be better, ma'am, to hear what Mr. Borrowdale wishes to tell you. I dare say it will not take long?' And he looked with a nervous smile into Simon's face.

'No; it will not take long,' Simon agreed smiling. 'If you would conduct your client to

161

her seat—?'

With a scornful look, the countess turned away and went back to her chair. Mr. Begby followed, looking relieved.

Mr. Borrowdale now wheeled round to the viscount and Kate. 'My lord, Miss Katherine, pray forgive me. But now, I beg leave to present to you one who has accompanied me from Italy.'

'Of course. if he has anything to do with the case, bring him in at once.'

'I thank you, my lord.'

Kate went to pull the bell-rope.

The countess now said in a very haughty voice, 'I really can not think why you imagine I should be interested in meeting this person, sir!'

'Ah, ma'am!' Mr. Borrowdale turned back to the countess. 'When you see—this person—I think you will be very interested indeed. The person is—er—an old acquaintance of yours.'

'I told you, I have no wish to meet any acquaintance from Italy!'

'Ah, ma'am, this is a very particular old acquaintance. One to whom, indeed, you were very—nearly related!' And Mr. Borrowdale smiled broadly as though at a secret joke.

The footman had now come and been given orders to show in Mr. Borrowdale's companion. At this moment, the door opened again, and the footman announced in impassive tones, 'The marchesa de Rocco

Santo.'

Kate herself gasped as a tall, dark woman entered the room, and the girl stole a quick look at Mr. Borrowdale. Then she turned back to regard the newcomer. The woman was wearing a frogged green travelling dress, and a broad-brimmed hat adorned with sweeping ostrich feathers. Her shining black hair was caught at the back of her head, and her look was imperious as she paused on the threshold, regarding each person in the room. Her brilliant eyes flickered a little as she caught sight of the countess, but otherwise she gave no sign of recognition.

Mr. Borrowdale hurried towards her, and caught her hand. She smiled at him gravely, and Mr. Borrowdale said, 'My dear, may I present Lord Netley, and Miss Katherine Netley. My lord, Miss Katherine, may I present the marchesa de Rocco Santo—my wife!'

'Your wife!' Kate burst out.

Mr. Borrowdale smiled proudly and nodded.

'Oh, ma'am!' Kate curtsied. 'Welcome! Welcome!' She turned back to Mr. Borrowdale. 'I am so happy for you, sir!'

The viscount greeted the marchesa, and while this was going forward, Kate eyed the Italian woman. She was tall, taller even than Kate herself, and very handsome in a brilliant way. But the most striking thing about her was the look of melancholy in her eyes, which only dissipated for a moment when she smiled at Mr. Borrowdale. Otherwise, she was quite grave, and seemed to emit an aura of sadness. Kate was puzzled. She could not think the marchesa had at all the look of a new bride.

When the greetings were done, the marchesa turned slowly to the countess. 'So, Marguerite; we meet again,' she said quietly, in her fluent if heavily accented English.

The countess had gone very pale when the Italian woman first entered the room. Now she rallied somewhat, and essayed a welcoming smile. 'Why! Maddalena! What a delightful surprise!' And she rose and made to come forward to kiss the other woman.

But the marchesa drew back abruptly. 'Keep away from me!' She looked scornfully at the other woman. 'Seeing you again is no delight for me!'

The countess shrugged. 'You never did like me, I know, Maddalena. You never wished me to be your sister. You did everything you could to stop it.'

'You never *were* my sister!' the marchesa returned in scathing tones. 'You cheated and lied to my poor Federigo, but—you were never, thank God, his wife!'

The countess smiled smugly. 'Ah! But the Marchese Federigo de Rocco Santo wished it with all his heart! It is unfortunate that—'

'Why! You—! You—!' The marchesa raised

164

an arm as if she would strike the countess, who backed away quickly.

Now Mr. Borrowdale stepped forward swiftly, and caught his wife's hand again in his. 'Calmly, my dear. Calmly. And my friends do not yet know the whole story. Would not it be best if you told them? As yet they are ignorant of everything.'

The marchesa passed her free hand wearily across her eyes, and smiled sadly at her husband. 'You are quite right, Simon. For a moment—I forget myself. The sight of this— this cattiva scroccona—brings everything back too clearly.'

'I know, my dear. I know.' Mr. Borrowdale put one hand on the marchesa's shoulder and looked at her anxiously. 'If you would prefer to wait a little—?'

The marchesa shook her head vehemently. 'No, no! I am quite well to say what I must say. What I have come to England to say!'

Kate, who up to now had been watching, fascinated by the Italian noblewoman, now remembered her duties as a hostess. 'Will not you be seated, Madame?'

The marchesa shook her head. 'I thank you, no. I am very well as I am.' She turned to look at the countess again. 'So, you are up to your old tricks I hear, signora.'

'Contessa, Maddalena. I am the Contessa Snaguingrazzo now.'

The marchesa's eyebrows rose

contemptuously. 'Pah! That old libertino! You have descended a long way from my Federigo!'

'Nevertheless, he was a count, and suited me very well.'

'I make no doubt he did!' the marchesa returned scathingly. 'Indeed, I would call it—a very suitable match! But—I am not come here to bandy words with you, signora—Oh! I beg your pardon—contessa!' she added sarcastically. 'I am come to England to tell what you did to my Federigo!'

The countess smiled complacently. 'It was all a long time ago, Maddalena.'

'Two years. But to me it seems but yesterday! And from how many other states have you been thrown out? You know what would happen if you returned to Genova! I suspect that you must be running short of hiding-places!'

The countess's eyes flashed at that, and she turned to her lawyer. 'I hope you note what is said, Begby. There may well be an action for slander that I shall wish to bring.'

'Trust me, countess. I am all attention.'

'Ah! So you have a dog with you still!'

The two women glared at each other, the countess with rising colour, the marchesa even paler than she had been before for all the darkness of her skin.

'My love!' Mr. Borrowdale now interposed. 'We await still! Will not you begin your story?'

'Oh! Yes, yes! I begin, I begin.' The

marchesa turned to Kate and her father. 'Milord Netley, Miss Katherine, some two years ago this woman, Marguerite Belleville, came to Genova. She brought with her introductions from some of the greatest families of Parma and Torino and Milano—to the best—the highest families of Genova. Among these there was one to the Rocco Santo family.' The marchesa broke off for a moment, then added quickly, 'I can tell you now, milord, Miss Katherine, that those letters were forged—all forged! False! Not one was genuine. But, at the time, we did not think . . . we accepted this woman, widowed, as we believed, and took her into our houses.'

As the marchesa spoke, the countess had risen and was edging towards the door. The others did not see her, but Mr. Borrowdale, alert, did, and now he stepped forward swiftly, and caught her by the wrist in a grip of steel. 'Oh, no, madam! You wait to hear the whole!'

'Let me go! Let me go!' The countess twisted like an eel.

'Not till we have what we want!' Mr. Borrowdale returned with a dangerous smile.

The countess glared at Mr. Borrowdale, and after a moment allowed him to lead her back to her chair, where she sat down with an ill grace.

The marchesa watched, smiled briefly at her husband, then continued. 'My brother, the young marchese de Rocco Santo, was then a youth of twenty. Only twenty. He met this woman, Marguerite Belleville, and fell head over heels in love with her. Oh, she was very beautiful—it was but natural. But what was not was that he must marry her. A woman old enough to be his mother!'

'It's a lie! I am but twenty-eight!' the countess cried now.

'Twenty-eight!' The marchesa turned on the other woman. 'Twenty-eight! You have been twenty-eight, signora, for nearly twenty years!'

The countess let out a cry, and screamed again that it was a lie.

The marchesa turned back to Lord Netley and Kate, and flung out her hands in an imploring gesture. 'I ask you, milord, Miss Katherine, only think! The head of the Rocco Santo family marrying—an adventuress! We did not know this then, of course. We thought only that she was too old to bear him an heir.'

The countess cried out again, but the marchesa took no notice. 'We pleaded with him—with Federigo. We begged him to consider how it would be in a few years time— to be saddled with an old wife. We begged him to consider the family, the name—how it must not be allowed to die out. But—he would listen to nobody. Nobody!' Tears came into the marchesa's voice, and she had to stop speaking for a moment.

Mr. Borrowdale was still standing by the countess's chair. He looked across at his wife

168

with concern.

She caught his glance, and smiled. Plainly, it was an effort, and the smile was sad, the merest curling of the corners of the full, red lips. 'You need not worry, Simone. I am quite well.' The Italian woman turned back once more to Kate and her father. 'Impetuously, my beloved little brother married this—creature—this—this—snake-in-the-grass. For six months she went about Genova bearing the once proud, noble, honourable name of Rocco Santo! She—a nobody! Soon, oh, very soon, we see what she is! What we have always known she must be. She take everything from my brother: jewels, money, deeds to land—all are taken by her, are put into her name. In six months, she is a rich woman—rich with the Rocco Santo fortune! My brother hardly speaks to us—his family. He knows how we feel about this woman, but to him—she is the only woman in the world—an angel. He can not see that she is bleeding him dry. He will hear nothing against her. Nothing! And if he knows that one has spoken ill of her, then he cuts that person out of his life as if he had never been. His own mother—he refused to see her. Our mother—died of a broken heart.'

The marchesa's face took on an expression of extreme sadness, and when she spoke next, her voice was only just audible. 'For six months life went on like this. As I have said, his own mother could do nothing. My uncles, in vain

169

they tried to reason with him. Our lawyers—
but he dismissed them. Nothing would stop my
brother giving everything to this—this
creature.'

Everyone in the room, but the marchesa,
was silent now. When she paused in her
speech, one might have heard a feather drop.

'We had tried to find out something of this
woman. We wrote to the senders of those
letters of introduction. They wrote back to say
that Marguerite Belleville was quite unkown to
them. But by then, it was too late. She was
already married to my poor brother. But then,
a family friend who had gone to Verona, came
back to Genova with the news that there was a
Joseph Belleville in prison in that city—for
cheating, stealing. After all our efforts, we had
a clue at last! Our lawyers hurried to Verona,
and spoke to this man. He was Marguerite
Belleville's husband, and very much alive. She
was, therefore, not married to our brother at
all! But was guilty of the crime of bigamy! Our
lawyers returned to Genova, ready to indict
her, but somehow this woman learnt of what
they had found, and when we went to confront
her- she had fled, taking with her all the jewels
and money she could carry.'

Kate had hardly taken her eyes off the
marchesa's face as the Italian spoke. Now she
looked towards the countess, horror and
loathing fighting for supremacy in her
thoughts. But the countess showed no

remorse. Rather, she looked defiant, and, somehow, triumphant.

'My poor brother would not believe anything of this at first. He was convinced a mistake had been made. Indeed, he refused to listen. He tried to follow her, but he could find no trace of her. He knew not which way she had taken. He returned home, still refusing to hear one word against her. He shut himself up in his room—he hardly ate—for days—weeks. Then he fell ill—fever weakened his body, and then his mind. He was in a delirium. He went mad with despair. And one night he climbed to the top of our chapel tower and threw himself from the parapet. We found him the *next* morning—lying dead on the flags beneath.'

The marchesa bent her head and her frame shook as if she were wracked with sobs. Then she raised her head again and stared at the countess as the tears ran down her cheeks. 'That woman murdered my brother—as surely as if she had stabbed him to the heart with a dagger!'

It was the countess who broke the silence which ensued when the marchesa had finished her story. 'It was indeed very sad,' she said nonchalantly. 'I was very much affected when I heard. But, I really can not be held responsible for what Federigo did! He was a very foolish, headstrong boy!'

'Is that all you can say—you who have murdered him?' the marchesa cried passionately. 'Oh, yes! He was a foolish boy! He was foolish to love you! He was foolish to believe you—you who know only how to lie. But he did not deserve to die!' The marchesa allowed the tears to fall for some moments, unhindered. Mr. Borrowdale made as if to come to her, but she held up her hand to forbid him.

Then the marchesa had regained her self-command. 'And now, I hear, you think to dupe some other man—the friend of my husband. If you do anything, anything at all, signora, I shall tell the world how you treated my Federigo—how you killed him—how you dare not show your face in Genova or Parma or Torino or Milano—or Verona—where you left your husband to rot in prison for your own thefts!'

The countess leaned back in her scat and smiled calmly. 'Do your worst, Maddalena! Tell all the world! It is your own brother who would come out as a fool—moon-calf that he was. I have nothing to fear from your words!'

Kate looked from one woman to the other, and with a heavy heart knew that what the countess said was true. She might be wanted in Genoa for the crime of bigamy, but here in England, she was still free. Her lies, her cheating, her stealing would not take her to prison here, for crimes committed in other states.

Now the countess sat up straight, as if

preparing to depart. 'Now, is that all?' she enquired in a bright social voice. 'I have heard Maddalena out, Mr. Borrowdale, as you requested. Now, perhaps, you will permit me to leave?' And she drew down her veil in a final gesture.

Mr. Borrowdale's face showed bafflement. He stared down at the countess for a moment, then stepped back, to allow her to pass him.

She rose and gave him a little bow. Then she looked across at Lord Netley. 'The next edition, my lord. That is my last word. Come Begby.' And giving a triumphant glance round at them all, the countess moved towards the door with great assurance.

As Kate watched her, she felt tears start to her eyes.

She knew that she must make her father do what the countess demanded; it must not be through her that Lord Barnstaple was made a subject for scandal.

If Lord Barnstaple did not return to face the countess—well; at least Kate would know that she had done all she could.

At the door the countess paused, waiting for Mr. Begby to open the door for her. The lawyer bowed quickly to those present, and hurried after the countess, clutching his lawyer's case under his arm.

He had just put his hand upon the handle to open it, when the handle was twisted out of his hand, and the door was flung open, knocking him backwards, and a great Irish voice roared, 'By St. Patrick, Marguerite! So I have come upon ye at last!'

CHAPTER TEN

At the sound of the voice, the countess went white, and it seemed that she must fall. The next moment, a giant of a man strode into the room, dressed in stained and dusty travelling clothes, his hair which must once have been red, now grizzled with white, but his luxuriant mustachios still showing the same colour as in youth.

The big man strode up to Marguerite and clasped her to him. 'Now then, my little white flower, what is this I have been hearing about ye?'

'Joseph!' the countess gasped faintly.

To say that the others in Lord Netley's library were taken aback is to put the matter very indifferently. Lord Netley himself gaped unashamedly. So did Mr. Borrowdale. Kate herself believed afterwards that she had done so, and even the marchesa showed complete astonishment. Only Mr. Begby had other matters on his mind as he picked himself up from the heap on the floor where the sudden opening of the door had deposited him.

The entrance of Marguerite Belleville's

husband, however, was only the first surprise. He was followed a moment later by another figure, also travel-stained and decidedly weary, but wearing a broad smile of satisfaction on his countenance, which lightened still more as his eyes fell upon Kate.

'My—my lord!' the girl gasped, hardly able to believe her eyes. She held out one hand tentatively, as though the figure might suddenly vanish. 'Oh, my lord!'

The figure came up to her and gripped both her hands in his. 'Kate! I am returned, you see, with the best means of all to overturn the countess's plans!'

'But—how? Where?' she gasped, incoherent still.

But the earl was looking about the room. He bowed to Lord Netley, then caught sight of Mr. Borrowdale and went over to him and the two men shook hands warmly. 'Simon!' Lord Barnstaple cried. 'How long have you been returned?'

The two men spoke for some moments, their pleasure in each finding the other safe plain for all to see.

Then Mr. Borrowdale introduced his wife, and it was the earl's turn to gape. He covered it very well, bowing most elegantly to the marchesa, and clapping Simon on his good shoulder and calling him a fast fellow, and demanding to know how it had come about. But there was no time for that just then, for

Joseph Belleville, who had been talking all the while to his wife, in what was for him a low voice, and which had, in fact, been swamped by the exclamations of the others in the room, now let out a roar.

'Ye foolish critter, ye, flower! And isn't it the best offer we shall ever have? All our debts paid, and a new start in a new world!'

'But—I have no wish to go to America, Joseph!'

'Wish it or no, that's where we're going! Ye're my wife, woman, and ye'll follow where I say!'

For a moment the countess—or as from henceforth she must be named, Mrs. Belleville, looked as if she would refuse. She glared up at her husband, her eyes blazing with anger. But Joseph Belleville smiled down at her, and suddenly his wife's face also broke into a smile. 'Very well, Joseph.'

'That's better now!' the man cried in a hearty voice. 'That's my little white flower! And haven't I been without ye too long to be without ye again?' Then Joseph Belleville turned to Lord Barnstaple. 'I'll be very happy to accept yer Lordship's offer for my wife and myself.' And he held out his hand.

At once Lord Barnstaple went over to him and took it. 'Good man!' He took from the pocket of his coat then a packet and a bag which was obviously full of money. Joseph Belleville held out his hand to take them, but

176

Lord Barnstaple said, 'I need—certain documents in return.'

'I had not forgot, my lord,' the Irishman smiled. Then he turned to his wife. 'I collect, flower, that ye have kept certain papers which, as I told his lordship with me hand on me heart, I had no idea ye had still. I have promised his lordship that he shall have them back. Every last one o' them.' And he looked down into his wife's eyes with a meaning look.

'I—I don't know what you mean, Joseph!'

'Oh, come, flower; ye know very well, I'm thinking. Certain—letters—now? Does that remind ye?'

Marguerite Belleville gazed up into her husband's face. What she was thinking, or what she was trying to see there could only be guessed.

Her husband said softly, 'Without the letters, flower, his lordship will not give us a penny, and I should not like to see yer pretty little head in the Marshalsea, for it's gone the last time that I take the blame for the two of us.' And he smiled down broadly.

'Very well, Joseph,' Mrs. Belleville said after a moment. Then turning to her lawyer, she said, 'Give Lord Barnstaple the documents, Begby.'

Mr. Begby, who had been quietly massaging the bruised portions of his anatomy while the foregoing was taking place, now picked up his case, took out the papers in it, and presented them to the earl with an ingratiating smile and an unnecessarily deep bow.

Lord Barnstaple took the sheets, and looked through them. His eyebrows rose as he looked, and when he had finished, he said to Mrs. Belleville, 'I congratulate you, madam. You have been busy indeed.'

Marguerite Belleville smiled. 'I believe in taking trouble if what I want is worth the candle.'

The earl bowed. 'I am flattered,' he said ironically. 'But—there seems to be something missing yet.'

'I assure you, Richard, you have them all. Unless something remains in Begby's case. Begby, pray examine your case to see if anything can have remained behind.'

'I assure you, my lady—er—ma'am, that—'

'Nevertheless, pray look, Begby.'

Mr. Begby did as he was bid, and went to the extent of showing the assembled company that his case was indeed now quite devoid of contents.

The earl uttered a sigh. 'I greatly regret, Belleville, but—if you are unable to complete your part of the bargain—'

Joseph Belleville turned back to his wife. 'His lordship is not satisfied, flower. Ye hear that? Now, we would not wish to upset such a kind gentleman as his lordship who is prepared to do so much for us, would we?'

'There is nothing more, Joseph. Richard is

mistaken.'

Belleville looked across at the earl who shook his head slightly.

The Irishman then turned back to his wife. Suddenly one hand shot out and grasped her by the wrist so that she winced with pain. 'I think it is ye who are mistaken, flower. Mr. Begby clearly has given his all, but—' The man paused and looked at his wife.

'You are hurting me, Joseph!'

The man's other hand shot out then and seized hold of his wife's reticule, and tugged it till the thin silken handle broke.

'Now, let us see what we have in here,' Joseph Belleville went on, his voice menacingly silky. He used both hands to open the little bag, and forcing in his huge fingers, he poked about and eventually pulled out a piece of paper. He held it up. 'Would this be what we're wanting now?'

Mrs. Belleville was rubbing her arm sulkily. She did not answer.

Joseph Belleville held it out to Lord Barnstaple who took it in his free hand, flicked it open with his thumb, and read swiftly.

'This is indeed it, Belleville,' he said after a moment. 'Though I confess to feeling a little unease that there may be others I know not of.'

'Now, don't let yer lordship worry,' Belleville said with easy reassurance. 'Isn't it my word ye're getting that all that's done with and in the past? Yer lordship won't be troubled again, I promise ye.'

Lord Barnstaple held out the packet and the bag of coins. 'I hope there will be no mistake, Belleville.'

The Irishman took the items from the car]. 'Oh, sure and there'll be no mistake, yer lordship; *I'll* see to that.' He turned to his wife. 'See this, flower. How kind his lordship is? How generous? Now, we wouldn't want to upset such a kind and generous gentleman, would we?'

Mrs. Belleville shot a glance of loathing at the earl, then looked at her husband sulkily. He caught her wrist again, and stroked the flesh which he had bruised a moment earlier. Suddenly she broke into a smile. 'No, Joseph; we certainly wouldn't!'

'That's better, my flower. And now, it's enough time we've taken up here.' Joseph Belleville addressed the others in the room. 'Ye'll forgive us, I'm certain, if we leave ye now. My wife and I have a long journey before us, and several little matters of business to attend to before we leave.' He bowed with a flourish to Lord Netley. 'My lord.' He turned to Kate and bowed even more floridly. 'Miss Katherine.' He bowed then to the marchesa and Mr. Borrowdale, and nodded to Mr. Begby. Then he offered his wife his arm.

Mrs. Belleville dropped one deep curtsy, a mocking smile on her face, then she took her husband's arm. Looking back over her shoulder she gazed at the earl for a moment, gave a little laugh and a small wave, and was swept from the room by the huge Irishman.

There was a short silence when the door closed behind them. Then Mr. Begby cried anxiously, 'I must depart also, my lord. Pray do excuse me.' And picking up his now empty case he bowed severally to them all, and backed to the door and somehow got out of the room, still uttering fulsome apologies.

It was Kate who began to laugh first, but her mirth was infectious, and soon all of them were in various states of hilarity except the marchesa, and even she was smiling quite broadly.

'Oh, my lord!' Kate gasped at last.' Pray do tell us what occurred—how you found the countess's—no! Mrs. Belleville's husband. She was never the countess Snaguingrazzo at all!'

'Indeed, she was not!' the earl returned, endeavouring to be calm.

'Twice she committed bigamy!' the marchesa cried. 'Oh, she is the most terrible woman!'

All except Lord Barnstaple knew the story of the marchesa's brother, and at once sobered up. His lordship saw the change in those about him, and became grave at once. He whispered to Kate, 'There is something I should know?'

'I will tell you later, my lord,' she whispered back.

'Well,' Lord Netley said now, 'after the dramas of today I am in distinct need of a restorative.' He went to the bell and tugged it, and looked round at them all. 'Brandy, gentlemen?'

The footman came at once and was sent to bring brandy and ratafia for the ladies. And then Lord Barnstaple was urged to tell how he had come upon Joseph Belleville.

'It was by the merest chance. I reached Genoa' The earl looked at Kate, who nodded.

'But there I completely lost your trail, Simon. I went to every hotel in the city, but could find no trace of you.'

'That was because my accident happened just after I had arrived. I had not gone to any hotel,' Mr. Borrowdale put in.

'I did not know what to do then, but thought you must have gone to Florence. Accordingly I continued my journey, and reached Spezia. There I had a piece of luck such as one can never count upon, but which can make all the difference between success and failure. I met an old acquaintance, a doctor from the University of Padua. He had been to Pisa and was returning home, and had journeyed from Pisa to Spezia by sea. He had missed the boat he meant to take, due to some mischance—he overslept, I think. Anyway, he was in Spezia at the time I was there myself, otherwise, I should never have seen him. I told him why I was in Italy, and though he could give me no news of you, Simon, he was able to tell me that one Joseph Belleville was still in prison in Verona. He knew this because my friend had happened to be in Verona, it is not far from Padua, when Belleville had been on trial, and it seems that it was a popular pastime to attend the court. My friend was certain he would have heard if Belleville had been released. It was quite a cause celebre at the time in that part of Italy.'

The footman came then with the wine and brandy, but as soon as everyone was served, and the servant had retired, Lord Barnstaple continued. 'I asked him if he was certain, for I had heard that Joseph Belleville was dead, but my friend was quite sure that he was still in the Werona gaol, and so I hurried to that city, and there found him.' The earl looked at the others wryly. 'It cost me a good deal of money, and several days before I could secure Belleville's release. We then hurried to England as fast as we could. I—I made a bargain with the man: I promised to pay his debts and to buy him and his wife a passage to America, and provide sufficient money for them to set themselves up there, on condition that I received back positively all the letters I had ever sent his wife, and that the two of them never attempted to return to Europe again. I—I confess, I shall feel safer knowing that the Atlantic is between myself and Marguerite Belleville.'

There were a great many more explanations then—from the earl, and from Simon, who told how he had met the marchesa through the surgeon who had cared for him when he had broken his arm, and from the marchesa, and from Kate herself, who told of her worry when no messages came from either the earl or Mr. Borrowdale.

The party did not break up till it was time for dinner, and Lord Netley insisted upon the earl and Mr. Borrowdale and the marchesa returning to dine in Wimpole Street; 'for there are still a great many matters I am not clear upon, and I dare say we all feel the same.'

*   *   *

The earl was in his dressing-room in Cavendish Square, being shaved once more by the faithful Jameson, who was delighted to see his master returned. Lord Barnstaple, thankful to be home again, with all his troubles behind him, was confiding to his valet a good many of the anxieties he had undergone, when a footman came to announce that the earl's lawyer, Mr. Banstead, was below.

'Banstead! Here! Oh, pray show him up!' Lord Barnstaple said, unable to imagine why the lawyer should wish to see him at that time.

Mr. Banstead of Banstead, Chipstead, Ashstead and Caterham, entered the earl's dressing room with something less than his usual urbanity. Both worry, and his recent hurrying upstairs, combined to render him somewhat short of breath.

'Well, Banstead! This is a surprise!'

'My lord! I should not have dreamt of disturbing your lordship at this time, but—I really felt that I must hear from your lordship's own lips that—Mr. Banstead paused to catch his breath.

'Yes?' The earl, his face now fit to show to the world once more after the ministrations of Jameson, wiped his face with the towel that had been under his chin, and stood up, and peered at himself in the glass closely. Jameson, good servant that he was, tactfully retreated out of earshot.

'My lord,' Mr. Banstead said, with a degree of calm, 'an—individual has been to see me.'

'Oh, yes?'

'By the name of Belleville, my lord.'

'Yes. I told him to wait upon you.'

'He had a letter from your lordship, bidding me see to the payment of certain bills—debts, I collect, incurred by this—Belleville, and begging me to furnish him with a certain sum of money—'

The earl who had been listening quietly, suddenly swung round. 'Asking for money, you say!'

'You had bid me give this man three hundred pounds, my lord.'

'Three hundred pounds!

'Here is the letter, my lord.' And Mr. Bansead handed over a sheet of paper.

Frowning, Lord Barnstaple took it, and read it through. 'Did you pay over the money, Banstead?'

'In view of the urgency lord, I thought it best to do so. The individual had, I collect, to catch a boat for America.' The lawyer stared at the earl's face narrowly. 'I regret, my lord, if I have done wrong—'

'No, no, Banstead; not wrong at all. Was that all?'

'No, my lord; it was not. The—er— individual left with me the counterfoils of the—the debts I collect you had agreed to clear. Before I can consent to pay them, my lord, I felt I should have your lordship's assurance that they were all in order. The sum, my lord, seems very great.'

'I did give Belleville a letter to take to you, bidding you see to the payment of his debts. The sum, I believe is some thousands—four or five.'

'The precise sum, my lord, is twenty-three thousand, four hundred and sixty-two pounds, nine shillings and sevenpence.'

The earl stared, then sat down again. 'Twenty-three thousand—'

'—four hundred and sixty-two pounds, nine shillings and sevenpence. The individual kindly remarked that I might leave off the halfpenny,' Mr. Banstead added after a moment.

'Did he indeed!' the earl ejaculated. He glanced at Mr. Banstead who was looking somewhat censorious. Then suddenly he began to chuckle. 'You have done quite right to come to me, Banstead, but—the matter is indeed correct. I agreed to pay this Belleville's debts, and I shall do so, though I had no idea the sum would be quite so large.'

Mr. Banstead rose. 'It is a weight off my shoulders, my lord. Three hundred pounds, though a large sum, is—not in the same league.'

'No, indeed.' Lord Barnstaple rose also.

'Now that you are returned to England, my lord, I dare say you will be arranging your wedding soon?' the lawyer asked tactfully.

'As soon as may be, Banstead. I may get a licence for next week!' the earl smiled.

'I am glad to hear it, my lord. Your late uncle would be very pleased.'

'Yes. He's got his way at last.'

'I trust you do not regret it, my lord?'

Lord Barnstaple surveyed the lawyer for a moment in silence. Then he smiled. 'You know, Banstead, I do not! In fact, I want nothing more now than to be safely married to Miss Netley. Indeed, if she would agree to it, I would marry her tomorrow!'

Mr. Banstead shook the earl's hand. 'My lord, I am delighted to hear it! Nothing could give my greater pleasure. Miss Netley is a charming young woman, and will make you an excellent wife, I am sure. Good family. Good stock, there. Yes; your late uncle would be very pleased.' The lawyer nodded, then broke into a smile. 'In view of what you have just told me, my lord, I feel I can let you into a little secret.'

'Secret?'

'Your late uncle, my lord, never intended to disinherit you!'

'What do you mean?' the earl gasped.

'Just that, my lord. The late earl bade me to tell you that it would happen were you not married at the end of one year after his death in order to bring you to the starting post. But—he never meant to do it.' And Mr. Banstead beamed from ear to ear.

'Never intended to—' the earl spluttered, his face wrathful. 'Do you mean to tell me, Banstead, that all this—this vexation and trouble I have been put to to find myself a bride—was unnecessary?'

'Yes, my lord!' Clearly Mr. Banstead thought it a good joke.

'Of all the—'

'Oh, do not blame my old friend, my lord! Your late uncle was anxious only for you to be happy. He always said you just needed a little push to get you moving!'

'A little push!' Lord Barnstaple was almost past speech now.

Still beaming, Mr. Banstead nodded. 'He was convinced you would be happier married than not, my lord. Oh, I know there was some little difficulty, years ago, my lord. Your uncle confided in me the gist of the matter. But— that was all long ago. His little ploy, my lord, was only a ruse to encourage you to screw your courage to the sticking-place, so to speak. He knew you would choose well.' And Mr. Banstead smiled blandly.

The earl glared at the lawyer, whose smile did not flinch. 'I am not at all sure, Banstead, that I should not remove my affairs to the care of another lawyer!' Lord Barnstaple exploded, but only mock angrily now.

'Ah, my lord; I should regret that greatly.'

'And so should I, Banstead,' Lord Barnstaple said after a moment, his face suddenly smiling as he held out his hand. 'So should I!'

*   *   *

During and after the dinner in Wimpole Street that evening, all those concerned told every detail they knew of the affair, till not one of them had any further questions to be satisfied. And when that subject was done, then nothing would content the earl but that he must have a very exact description once more of how his friend had come to be married so unexpectedly.

It was not very late when the party broke up, for Mr. Borrowdale and his bride meant to travel that night to Mr. Borrowdale's mamma's home in the country, and when the pair had departed, Lord Netley discreetly, and perhaps with some relief, withdrew to his study to continue his contemplation of his new prints which had been interrupted, it seemed, so long ago.

Kate and Lord Barnstaple were left alone in the salon.

'Well, my lord?' Kate smiled.

'Well, Kate?'

'I am thankful you are come home safe, my lord. I feared so much.'

'And Simon also. I was right to worry, you see. He had met with an accident!'

'But one which had a very happy outcome, my lord!'

The earl laughed. 'I should never have believed I should see Simon Borrowdale married—and before myself!' He smiled at Kate. 'Shall we follow them soon?'

'It might be as well, my lord,' Kate managed to answer lightly; 'before any further difficulties intervene!'

'I am not afraid of anything else—now that Marguerite Belleville is to put the Atlantic between us. By the by, there is one thing, Kate, which I did not mention to the others earlier.'

'And what is that, my lord?'

'Marguerite Belleville succeeded in playing one last trick upon me,' the earl said ruefully.

'How, my lord?' Kate cried, all indignation.

'I gave Belleville a letter for Banstead, my

lawyer, in which I directed Banstead to pay Belleville's debts. He was to take the letter to Banstead's chambers, together with the chits for his debts. Well, by the time the letter was handed to Banstead, an addition had been made.'

'Saying what, my lord?'

'Asking Banstead to hand over to Belleville the sum of three hundred pounds.'

'Three hundred pounds! But—are not you going to stop them, my lord!'

'It is a small enough sum, compared with the whole I have been saddled with, Kate,' the earl returned wryly. Then he let out a chuckle and Kate looked at him enquiringly. 'You know, Kate, I can not *like* the Bellevilles, but— I can not help admiring their impudence!'

'I think they are both dreadful people!' Kate cried roundly. 'They are very well suited!'

'You are right there, Kate!'

'When I think—of all the trouble that woman has put you to—!'

Still chuckling, the earl said now, 'And do you know, Kate, what Mr. Banstead also told me! He told me that my late uncle had not the least idea of disinheriting me after all. That it was but a ruse to make sure that I did marry!'

Kate stared at the earl, and suddenly her heart was like lead in her breast. 'You mean, my lord,' she said falteringly, in a tiny voice, 'you mean—you wish to withdraw from our—

our arrangement?'

'Withdraw! Kate! What are you saying?' Lord Barnstaple seized Kate's hands. 'Of course, I do not wish to withdraw. Such a thought never entered my head! I just thought you might be amused to know that all the—'

But Kate had turned away her head, and would not meet the earl's eyes.

'Kate! What is this? Oh, my dear—dear Kate! What a fool I am! I did not think how it would seem to you—Oh, my dear—dearest girl—I want nothing more than to marry you! You must believe me, Kate!'

Slowly the girl turned to look at him, hesitating to believe what her ears told her the earl was saying.

'Listen to me, Kate!' Lord Barnstaple went on urgently. 'I know that, when we became betrothed, it was but a business arrangement for us both! But—during those weeks—I—I have changed, Kate. I have come, not only to value and admire you, Kate—but also—to love you. When I was in Italy, I could hardly wait to get back to you, Kate. The idea that I might ever have to marry that terrible woman nearly made me mad! I—I know that—I can not expect you to feel the same; I remember that it is but a short time ago that you had every hope of—of marrying another! But, in time, Kate,' the earl went on very wistfully now, 'in time, Kate, perhaps you could come to—to feel some affection for me?'

Kate stared at the earl, her heart thudding in her breast, and a beaming smile broke out upon her countenance. 'You—really love me, my lord?'

'With all my heart!'

The earl must have seen the reflection of Kate's feelings in her eyes. 'Kate!' he breathed. 'Kate, my dearest love! Do you mean—am I right—you mean—for me—you feel—?'

Kate nodded her head, laughing at the earl's pitiful attempts to say what he meant. 'Yes, my lord! I—do not know how it has happened, or when it happened, but—I also have found that I have—fallen in love—with *you*!'

'Oh, Kate! Kate!' The earl seized her hands and kissed them. Then he clutched them and looked at her, suddenly very determined. 'Kate! From the very beginning, something was always wrong. There are correct ways to go about things—and incorrect ways. And we started incorrectly. I mean to set that right at once!'

'My lord?' Kate gasped, completely at sea.

The earl dropped to one knee. '*I* mean to propose to you, ma'am, as I should have done at the very beginning. And I warn you, I shall expect a favourable reply! I shall not take no for an answer!'

'My lord!' Kate laughed; 'I promise you I will say exactly what you want me to say!'

We hope you have enjoyed this Large Print book. Other Chivers Press or G.K. Hall & Co. Large Print books are available at your library or directly from the publishers.

For more information about current and forthcoming titles, please call or write, without obligation, to:

Chivers Press Limited
Windsor Bridge Road
Bath BA2 3AX
England
Tel. (01225) 335336

OR

G.K. Hall & Co.
P.O. Box 159
Thorndike, Maine 04986
USA
Tel. (800) 223-2336

All our Large Print titles are designed for easy reading, and all our books are made to last.